Lily Rules!

Other Books in the Young Women of Faith Library

The Lily Series
Here's Lily!
Lily Robbins, M.D. (Medical Dabbler)
Lily and the Creep
Lily's Ultimate Party
Ask Lily
Lily the Rebel
Lights, Action, Lily!

Non-fiction
The Beauty Book
The Body Book
The Buddy Book
The Best Bash Book
The Blurry Rules Book
The It's MY Life Book
The Creativity Book
The Uniquely Me Book
Dear Diary
Girlz Want to Know
NIV Young Women of Faith Bible
YWOF Journal: Hey! This Is Me
Take It from Me

Young Women of Faith

Lily Rules!

Nancy Rue

Zonderkidz

Zonder**kidz**™

The children's group of Zondervan

www.zonderkidz.com

Lily Rules!
Copyright © 2002 by Women of Faith

Requests for information should be addressed to:

Zonderkidz, *Grand Rapids, Michigan 49530*

ISBN: 0-310-70250-X

Published in association with the literary agency of Alive Communications, Inc., 7680 Goddard Street, Suite 200, Colorado Springs, CO 80920.

Editor: Barbara Scott

Interior design: Amy Langeler

Printed in the United States of America

02 03 04 05/❖ DC/5 4 3 2 1

Chapter 1

All right, guys," Ms. Ferringer said shrilly into the microphone. "Let's settle down now. You guys in the back — take your seats — we need to get started."

Lily Robbins looked around her and shook her head of wildly curly red hair. "Like anybody's listening to her," she said to her best friend, Reni Johnson, who was sitting next to her in the auditorium.

Reni pursed her lips, popping out her dimples. "She might as well be talking to a bunch of animals," she said.

"She is."

Lily pointed to the small group of seventh graders who had been arranging themselves into seats three rows down for the last ten minutes. Ashley Adamson was trying to place everybody boy-girl, amid much flipping of turned-up blonde hair and rolling of heavily shadowed blue eyes. Her cohort, Chelsea Gordon, was plucking at the boys' shirtsleeves and laughing up into their faces — practically drooling as far as Lily could tell.

"She's gotta be the worst flirt in the whole seventh grade," said Zooey Hoffman, who was sitting on the other side of Lily.

On the other side of Zooey, Suzy Wheeler shook her head, her shiny, straight black hair splashing against her cheeks. "Bernadette's worse."

Lily had to strain to hear Suzy, who was obviously trying to follow Ms. Ferringer's instructions even though none of the other students were.

"What Suzy say?"

That came from Kresha Ragina, who was sitting on the other side of Reni, squinting from behind her wispy, sand-colored bangs.

This has got to be hard for Kresha, Lily thought.

Kresha was from Croatia, and although her English was improving all the time, she still had trouble sorting out words when there was chaos.

"She said Bernadette is the biggest flirt in the seventh grade," Reni told her.

"What is 'flirt'?"

Lily let Reni explain it to Kresha while she studied Bernadette. She was definitely tossing her head of shoulder-length, curling-ironed hair at Benjamin. But she had some pretty stiff competition from Chelsea and Ashley and about five other girls who were all snatching ball caps from the heads of boys who, they obviously knew, would go to great lengths to get them back.

What is so fun about being around a bunch of absurd little creeps? Lily thought. *Give me my Girlz anytime.*

She looked down the row on either side of her at Suzy, Zooey, Reni, and Kresha — the Girlz Only Club — and gave a contented sigh. Just then the microphone squawked with feedback up on the stage, which sent everybody into a frenzy of moaning and ear covering. Ms. Ferringer took that opportunity to shout, "Quiet down now, guys, or we won't get any class officers elected today."

At that, Ashley half-rose in her seat and made a loud shushing noise. The auditorium got as quiet as it was probably going to get.

"She *so* thinks she runs this school," Zooey whispered to Lily, round eyes rolling.

Lily rolled hers back and then settled into the seat. This was going to be a long assembly, watching the popular kids get elected to office. It was going to give them still another reason to act like they owned Cedar Hills Middle School.

"We're three months into the school year," Ms. Ferringer said into the mike.

"Ya think?" somebody in Ashley's row shouted.

A bunch of kids laughed. Lily didn't.

"And now that you've all had a chance to get to know people who've come here from other elementary schools, you get to elect officers."

"She talks like one of the kids," Reni whispered to Lily. "No wonder she doesn't have any control."

Lily nodded. Even now in the row in front of them, Daniel and Leo were launching folded-up pieces of paper from rubber bands.

"Here's how this is going to work, guys," Ms. Ferringer was shouting, even though she was practically swallowing the microphone at this point. "Quiet down, now—I will take nominations for president first."

Hands went up in Ashley's row, and somebody yelled out "Benjamin!" The rest of them clapped like the voting had already happened.

"If you nominate someone," Ms. Ferringer went on, "you have to give a nominating speech—not longer than a minute—about why you think your candidate would make a good officer."

Bernadette waved her hand more wildly than ever. Ms. Ferringer pointed to her, and Bernadette bounced out of her seat and up the aisle toward the stage, hair swinging down her back in perfect curls.

"I want to nominate Benjamin!" Bernadette squealed into the mike. Ashley's row erupted.

Ms. Ferringer paused, dry-erase marker in her hand. "What is Benjamin's last name?" she asked.

Bernadette looked at her as if she'd lost her mind. "Hel-lo-o," she said. "Weeks!"

7

"Like everybody in the world knows him," Reni muttered to Lily.

While Ms. Ferringer wrote Benjamin's name on the white board, Bernadette dazzled the auditorium with a smile and said, "I nominate Benjamin because — he's so cute!" Then she squealed again and tossed her hair. "No — just kidding — I mean, he *is* cute — but that's not why he should be president. He should be president because — like — who else knows as many people as he does?"

Ashley's row cheered as if Bernadette had just delivered the Gettysburg Address, and Bernadette bounced back to her seat.

"Any other nominations?" Ms. Ferringer said.

To Lily's surprise, Ashley raised her hand.

"Who's she gonna nominate?" Reni whispered to Lily. "I thought her whole crowd would be voting for Benjamin."

"Come on up," Ms. Ferringer said to Ashley. Although the auditorium was still one big squirming mass, she looked pleased, as if things were going rather well. Lily looked at the clock. They still had fifty endless minutes to go.

When Ashley got to the microphone, she took a few seconds to connect with her group, who all whistled and cheered before she even said anything. Then she leaned into the mike, gave a somewhat evil smile, and said, "I nominate Lily Robbins."

Lily immediately knew she was starting to blotch up like she always did when she wanted to crawl into a hole and die. Ashley would do *anything* to humiliate Lily.

"I think Lily Robbins should be president," Ashley was saying, still with that sarcastic smile on her face, "because she's, like, way responsible, and she's totally serious about everything." She paused, as if she were expecting boos. There were a few exaggerated snores and one shout of, "Oh — so she's a geek!" But it apparently wasn't enough for Ashley, because she added, "And she's teacher's pet in, like, every class."

That did it. The auditorium exploded with put-down laughter and cut-down comments. Lily felt like she was being sliced and diced for a trip to the frying pan.

"So if you like that kind of a person," Ashley shrieked over the commotion, "vote for Lily Snobbins — oh, sorry — Robbins."

"I'm gonna throw up," Lily said to Reni.

"Are you really?" Zooey said. "Do you want me to go to the restroom with you?"

"No!" Reni said. "You have to stay here and vote!"

"Like it's gonna matter," Lily said as she watched Ashley wiggle triumphantly back to her seat. "Nobody's gonna vote for me after that speech."

"Will the two candidates please hide your eyes?" Ms. Ferringer said from the stage. "We will vote by raising hands. Teachers — are you ready to count?"

Several of the teachers and administrators stood up, including Officer Horn, the school's policewoman, who was known among the students as Deputy Dog. Right now she was living up to her nickname as she came down the aisle and stood like a rottweiler at the end of Ashley's row.

"She's gonna make sure nobody raises more than one hand," Reni said. "Cover your eyes, Lily."

Lily did, gladly. There was no way she wanted to see how badly she was about to be defeated.

"All those for Benjamin raise your hands, please," Ms. Ferringer said.

Lily could feel arms waving in front of her and behind her. She could also hear Ashley's friends giving a victory whoop.

"All those for Lily —"

There was a lot of rustling around — more than Lily expected — and beside her, she heard Reni gasp.

"Lily!" she whispered. "I think you just won!"

Lily shook her head. "No way!" she whispered back.

There was a long, unbearable pause, and then Ms. Ferringer cried out, "Lily Robbins is our seventh-grade class president!"

She sounded as amazed as Lily felt. Lily pulled her hands away from her eyes and looked around, stunned. The first person she saw was Ashley, popping up out of her seat.

"That's not right!" she shouted. "We demand a—" She turned abruptly to her friends. "What's that thing called?" she said.

"A recount!" Benjamin called out.

Ms. Ferringer hesitated, as if she were considering it. Down in the front, Mrs. Reinhold—the English teacher—was shaking her head firmly. Ms. Ferringer glanced down at her and shook her head at Ashley.

"She's as scared of Mrs. Reinhold as we are!" Suzy said.

At least, that was what Lily *thought* Suzy said. She was still so flabbergasted, she wasn't sure of anything she was hearing.

But Ms. Ferringer erased Benjamin's name from the board and opened the nominations for vice president. Bernadette was, of course, on her feet at once, but Lily missed most of what went on for the next few minutes.

I'm president! was all she could think. *I'm president of the whole seventh-grade class!*

Visions of standing before them all, gavel in hand, filled Lily's head. She'd have to rethink her wardrobe, of course. You couldn't conduct class meetings in jeans. She'd definitely have to tame her hair—and probably get a more conservative binder since hers had Winnie the Pooh on the front. Then there were going to be bills and amendments to introduce and all that stuff that she wasn't quite sure about yet, but if she got some books to read about government and maybe interviewed the mayor—

She was imagining herself putting some important-looking document on the principal's desk when Reni nudged her and said, "Raise your hand!"

"Why?" Lily said, as Reni grabbed her wrist and jerked her arm into the air.

"You're voting for Ian Collins!"

"Who's Ian Collins?"

"I don't know — but he's not Benjamin!"

Lily looked with glazed eyes at the dry-erase board. The names Ian Collins and Benjamin Weeks had been written there, and votes were obviously being taken. It looked as if Benjamin's name was about to be erased again.

"Ian Collins is our winner!" Ms. Ferringer said — although she looked once more at Mrs. Reinhold for the final nod. Ashley's group stood up and chanted, "Recount!"

Lily ignored them and checked out Ian Collins, who was sitting across the aisle, being congratulated by his friends.

Oh, yeah, Lily thought. *I know him.* He was in a couple of her classes, but she'd never noticed him much, probably because he wasn't obnoxious. Most of her attention to boys had been attracted by the stupid things they always seemed to be doing.

Lily looked curiously at Ian. He was taller than a lot of the boys in seventh grade, most of whom still came up to about Lily's shoulder. He was skinny, and he wore his almost-blond hair short but not weirdly shaved anywhere, and he was currently grinning at a couple of his buddies, brown eyes shining from behind a pair of wire-rim glasses.

Yikes, Lily thought, *we elected somebody who wears glasses?*

That made her a little nervous, actually. If he wore glasses and he was still popular enough to get voted in, he must be pretty cool. Cool was never a word other kids used to describe Lily. She knew that. Working with Ian could be humiliating.

But Lily straightened her shoulders. *I'm president now,* she told herself. *It's all about confidence.*

Just then, Ian looked across the aisle and caught her eye. She gave him a quick wave. He grinned, and it wasn't an "oh, brother, I have to work with a dork" smile but one that said, "All right."

It was enough to inspire Lily to shoot her hand up when Ms. Ferringer said, "Nominations for secretary?"

"Suzy Wheeler," Lily said when Ms. Ferringer called on her. She could hear shy Suzy protesting as Lily rose to give her nominating speech, but Lily ignored her. Suzy was the neatest, most organized person on the planet, which was what Lily told her audience. When she was finished, Ashley's whole row stood up like one person and shouted, "Boo!"

Before Lily could even start to turn blotchy, Deputy Dog was on them, hauling the whole crowd of them out of their seats and up the aisle. When the vote was taken, there was barely anybody there to vote for their candidate, Chelsea. Suzy was elected by a landslide.

From there it was a piece of cake getting Ian's friend Lee Ohara elected treasurer and Zooey elected historian. Kresha gave an adorable speech about Zooey's experience with scrapbooking. Lily was convinced most people voted for Zooey because they thought Kresha's accent was cute. By the time the assembly was over, none of Ashley's crowd had been elected to office, and three of the five Girlz had.

It was the two who hadn't — Kresha and Reni — who made Lily play down her victory as they all headed off for their second-period classes. Reni and Kresha seemed happy for them, but it struck Lily that this was one of the few times they wouldn't all be doing something together.

Lily changed the subject to what they were all going to do at their Girlz Only Club meeting at Zooey's after school. She was sure that made Kresha's smile a little wider and Reni's dimples a little deeper.

By the time she got home that day, however, Lily was about to pop to really share the news in style with somebody. Mom and Dad, she knew, were going to be so proud. And besides, with her older brother

Art always winning at band contests and her little brother Joe hauling home trophies for every sport in life, it was nice to be a winner herself for a change.

She was a little disappointed when she first got home that Dad wasn't available. The Robbins family was adding on to the house — in preparation for a new kid they were hoping to adopt — and Dad was tied up in his study with a tattooed construction worker, poring over blueprints.

Mom didn't get home until almost 5:30, and by then Lily was ready to explode. She met Mom at the door from the garage, and said, "Guess what!"

"You got through the entire afternoon without getting into a fight with either of your brothers," Mom said. Her mouth twitched the way it did when she was teasing.

"No!" Lily said. "I mean — I did — but that's not my news."

"That's enough news for me," Mom said. "I may go into shock." She put two bags of groceries on the kitchen counter. "Help me get the rest of the stuff out of the car, would you, Lil?"

"Mom — wait — you hafta hear my real news!" Lily grabbed both of her mother's hands. "I was elected class president today!"

Mom gave the expected jolt of surprise, her brown-like-a-deer's eyes widening.

But then she pointed to one of the kitchen chairs and said, "Sit down, Lil. I think we need to talk about this."

Chapter
2

Lily felt herself deflating, kind of like a bicycle tire with a slow leak.
"Aren't you happy for me, Mom?" she said.

"Of course, I am," Mom said. There was a "but" coming, though. Lily could tell by the way Mom tightened her ponytail and then folded her hands on the tabletop.

"I just want you to think about this," Mom said. "You already have Girlz Only, plus you're going to want to be in the Shakespeare Club production again in the spring."

"But—"

"*And* you're still recuperating from pneumonia—and we have the adoption coming up—"

"But—"

"*Plus* you need time for studying and church activities." Mom gave Lily another long look. "I just don't want you spreading yourself too thin. You know how you go after things 200 percent."

"But I can do it all, Mom!" Lily said. "And this is, like, the most important thing that ever happened to me in my whole life!"

A voice from the doorway said, "Dude, did you win the lottery or something?"

Lily barely glanced at her sixteen-year-old brother Art who stuck his reddish-brown head in the refrigerator.

"I'm class president!" Lily said.

"On top of everything else she has going," Mom said.

Art pulled his head out, a container of salsa in his hand. "Don't worry about it, Mom," he said as he began to forage in a cabinet. "All the class president does in middle school is get her picture in the yearbook. By tomorrow everybody'll forget who it is."

"Okay, look," Mom said to Lily. "You and your father and I will sit down and talk about this and make sure this is something you should be taking on."

"Can we do it as soon as that construction guy leaves?" Lily said.

"No—I have dinner to get on the table." Mom pulled a bag of tortilla chips out of Art's hand. "That means no snacks."

"Tonight, then?" Lily said. She knew her voice was pleading—bordering on whining, even—but this was *way* important.

"Dad and I have a meeting at the adoption agency tonight," Mom said. "Now don't go ballistic on me—we'll get to it." She stood up. "You two go get the rest of the groceries out of the car."

Lily could feel her face blotching as she followed Art out the door.

"Don't start freaking out," Art said as they headed through the garage. "Like I said, it's not that big of a deal. You don't even do anything."

"Huh," Lily said.

Maybe class president used to be a job where you didn't do anything, but it wasn't going to be that way this year, not with her in office. This year, she was going to shake the whole place up—*if* Mom and Dad would let her.

After they left for their meeting that night, Lily holed up in her room with her talking-to-God journal and her dog Otto. He busied himself chewing on an old toothbrush he'd pulled out of the trashcan while Lily poured out her dilemma to God.

I think it was a miracle that I got elected, she wrote, *which means you meant for it to be. Please work on Mom and Dad so they'll see that. And please let me get along with that Ian kid, even though he's a boy. And please don't let Kresha and Reni feel left out. And please make me the best president of the seventh grade that ever was.*

Lily paused to consider that last request. From what Art had said, it wasn't going to be that hard to surpass everybody else who had ever held the office.

But I'm still going to be amazing, God, she wrote. *I just have to be positive.*

The next morning when Lily got to school, she headed straight for the bench by the stairs where she and the Girlz usually met before classes. She knew they'd be sympathetic.

No one else was there yet, and Lily had just pulled off her backpack when Deputy Dog strolled up, giving Lily a big, square grin.

"Congratulations, Robbins," she said, sticking out a hand for Lily to shake.

She pumped Lily's arm enthusiastically, but Lily barely noticed. Her mind was already forming the outline of an idea.

"I really want to make a difference while I'm in office," Lily said to her. "Maybe you could help me."

Deputy Dog folded her arms. "How so?" she said.

"Maybe we could get some rules changed that aren't really that fair."

Deputy Dog grunted, but she didn't hook her thumbs into her belt, which would have been the sign that she was getting mad.

"There are a few I'd like to see changed myself," Officer Horn said, "but most of them aren't made by the administrators here — they're set up by the county school board. We're talking about the big boys."

"Huh," Lily said.

Deputy Dog narrowed her eyes. "I know that look, Robbins."

"What look?" Lily said. She tried to get any look at all off of her face.

"That nobody's-going-to-stop-me look." Deputy Dog leaned closer to Lily. "You're a good kid. Don't go getting yourself in trouble, y'hear me?"

"There won't be any trouble," Lily said. "I'm going to do everything right."

Deputy Dog gave another soft grunt. "Maybe you better check with me before you do anything serious," she said. "I know Ms. Ferringer is your class advisor, but—"

She didn't finish the sentence. She didn't have to. Lily knew what she meant. Poor Ms. Ferringer had looked like she was going to collapse after yesterday's assembly.

Zooey, Suzy, and Kresha arrived then, and Deputy Dog sauntered away.

"What were you guys talking about?" Zooey asked.

Suzy knitted her delicate black eyebrows together. "Are you in trouble?"

Lily gave a nonchalant shrug. "We were just talking about class president stuff," she said. She stole a glance at Kresha. She was sure she saw something lonely flicker through her eyes. It was a bummer Reni didn't meet with them in the mornings, or Kresha would have had somebody who knew how she felt. But Reni practiced her violin in the orchestra room every day before school.

Just then, Lily saw Reni hurrying by, violin case in hand. Walking with her was a girl Lily had seen only a couple of times.

"Reni! Hi!" Kresha shouted.

Reni turned from her conversation with the other girl and smiled vaguely in their direction. Without stopping, she hurried on toward the music wing.

"Well, excuse me!" Zooey said.

"She not wave," Kresha said, forehead wrinkled.

"She was in a hurry," Suzy said. "She's late for practice."

Huh, Lily thought. *Reni's* my *best friend. What was she doing with that* other *girl?*

"That's Monique Masterson," Zooey said. "She's in the dumb classes with me."

While the other Girlz jumped on Zooey for calling herself dumb, Lily pushed the jealous pang out of her chest. She and Reni had been best friends forever, and they always would be. No need to worry.

In fourth period that day, Ms. Ferringer was supposed to give a geography test. When they arrived for class, however, she looked more nervous than any of the students. She was pulling everything out of her desk drawers and muttering to herself.

"What's with her?" Chelsea said, curling her lip.

"Who cares?" Ashley said.

But Marcie McCleary was happy to inform them. "She can't find her keys."

Lily tried not to look suspiciously at Marcie. The way she dressed these days, chains hanging from her jeans and fake tattoos dotting her arms, it made her a prime suspect when anything was missing. Marcie had teamed up with a bunch of gang wannabes at the beginning of the year and was always being called to the office for one thing or another.

Ms. Ferringer didn't bother to question Marcie or anybody else. When the bell rang she gave the bottom drawer of her desk one last inspection and then stood up and began frantically passing out test papers.

"Get out a pen or pencil," she said. The way her eyes were darting all around, Lily was sure she wouldn't have cared if they'd written in crayon.

"She's freaking," Reni whispered to Lily.

"What's so important about a bunch of keys?" Lily whispered back.

As soon as Ms. Ferringer had passed out the papers, she dove back to the desk and continued her search. Within seconds, she looked as if she'd forgotten there was even a class in the room.

Lily finished the test quickly, and even after she checked over all her answers twice, most of the other kids were still working. She noticed that on the other side of the room, Ian Collins had put his pencil down and was staring into space.

At least I have a smart vice president, Lily thought. She also thought about the note she'd gotten in first period from Ms. Ferringer, saying they would have an officers' meeting during lunch. Lily wished she could jot down some ideas, but that would mean getting stuff out of her backpack, and Ms. Ferringer wouldn't let them do that during a test. She at least tried to be strict about cheating.

So Lily leaned back in her seat and looked around to see if everybody was almost done. Reni was, and Suzy. Also Lee Ohara. Ashley, however, was still hard at it—pencil scratching across her paper. As Lily watched her, she stopped writing and slid her paper ever so slightly toward the edge of her desk.

It's gonna fall on the floor, Lily thought.

And then it did. Ashley didn't reach down to scoop it up, because Benjamin was too quick for her. He leaned down, grabbed the paper, held it up so he could brush the dirt off of it, and then slowly handed it to her.

Ashley gave him a sly smile as she took it back from him

Oh, brother, Lily thought. *She* so *did that on purpose!* She shook her head. There they were, in the middle of a test, and Ashley was flirting, right under Ms. Ferringer's nose.

Currently, Ms. Ferringer's nose was in the closet, where she was tossing stuff behind her, still muttering to herself. Ashley probably could have stood up and hugged Benjamin and Ms. Ferringer would have kept on looking for her keys.

Lily slid down in her desk and was about to go back to daydreaming about the upcoming officers' meeting when she saw Chelsea's paper fall off of *her* desk. Benjamin went after it and did the same routine as he'd done with Ashley's paper.

Best friends competing for the same boy, Lily thought. *What is the deal?*

Chelsea, it seemed, was willing to go a step further than Ashley. She leaned across the aisle and whispered something to Benjamin. Lily looked nervously at Ms. Ferringer, who was now on her hands and knees, peering around on the floor. She started to bring her head up, but she banged it on the underside of her desk.

"Who's talking?" Ms. Ferringer said. "You are taking a test!"

"Ya think?" Ashley murmured. But she and Chelsea and Benjamin and Bernadette locked their eyes on their papers, pictures of innocence, all of them. By the time Ms. Ferringer got to her feet, they were dotting their final i's.

"Time's up," Ms. Ferringer said. "Turn in your papers."

As tests made their way to the front, Lily couldn't help looking at Ashley and her friends again. They were wearing smiles so smug that they might as well have had "WE JUST TALKED DURING A TEST AND GOT AWAY WITH IT!" written across their foreheads.

Ms. Ferringer missed it. She was busy writing something on the board. THE SEMESTER PROJECT, it said.

"I hate doing those," Ashley said. "They're so lame."

"No problem," Benjamin said. He looked at Ashley and winked at her. She melted. *Ashley's now ahead by one flirt,* Lily thought.

"This is to be a full-length report on a country that you will draw out of a hat," Ms. Ferringer was saying. "Tomorrow I will give you an outline of what I want in it."

"If she can find it," Benjamin whispered.

Ashley and Chelsea laughed, and Ms. Ferringer looked at them blankly. Lily was starting to feel sorry for her.

"You'll have to include maps and sketches," Ms. Ferringer went on. "Don't wait until the last minute, because this is going to be worth half your grade."

Lily waited for Ashley and Benjamin and Bernadette and Chelsea — the ABCs — to protest. The girls looked at Benjamin, who winked at each of them this time. Then they all got that superior expression on their faces that made Lily squirm.

But Lily forgot about the four of them when the bell rang and everybody left for lunch except her and Suzy and Ian and Lee. Zooey hurried in a few minutes later, as Ms. Ferringer was instructing them to put their chairs in a circle. Lily could tell she was still thinking mostly about her keys, though, which was fine, because Lily was prepared to run the meeting anyway. She'd even covered her Winnie the Pooh binder with plain white paper the night before.

When they were all settled, Lily said, "The meeting will now come to order." She'd seen that on TV one time, and it seemed like an important thing to do. Of course, in this case, nobody was out of order to begin with, but Lily said to Suzy, "Write down everything that happens."

Suzy pulled a perfectly sharpened pencil out of the zipper pouch in her binder and went to work.

"I think the first order of business," Lily said — another thing she'd heard on TV — "should be to decide when we're going to meet. I think it should be once a week, only not after school because I have another meeting every day after school."

"I move we make it on Wednesdays," Ian said.

"You 'move'?" Zooey said. "What's that mean?"

Lily hoped Ian knew, because she didn't.

"It means I'm making a motion," Ian said.

"Oh," Zooey said. She blinked a couple of times.

"He's suggesting something," Ms. Ferringer told her. "Although I'm not sure we have to be that formal."

"I do," Lily said. "It'll keep us organized." Then she made a mental note to look up things like motions the first chance she got.

"You should ask if there's a second to my motion," Ian murmured to Lily.

"Oh, yeah," Lily said. "Is there a second to Ian's movement?"

"Motion," Ian whispered.

"I second it," Lee said.

Yikes, Lily thought. *I have a lot to learn!*

"Now you ask for all those in favor to say 'aye,'" Ian muttered to Lily.

"All those in favor say 'aye,'" Lily said.

Everybody said "aye," though Zooey was still looking confused.

"Your first motion has carried," Ms. Ferringer said. She seemed amused, but Lily ignored that. She'd see how serious they were pretty soon. "I'm glad you're all so enthusiastic," she went on, "but I don't think you have to meet that often."

"We do if we're going to make a difference," Lily said.

She was glad to see Ian nodding his head, along with Suzy and Zooey, of course.

"Well," Ms. Ferringer said, "I've been told that the only thing the seventh-grade class has to do is a fund-raiser to buy something for the school. Y'know — like new soccer balls or some computer software."

Lily felt herself deflating again.

"I've got an idea," Ian said. He looked at Lily. "Is it okay if I have the floor?"

"What does *that* mean?" Zooey said.

"It means I can talk," Ian said.

Lily could hear Suzy whispering as she wrote, "Ian has the floor."

"I think we should poll our constituents," Ian said. He looked at Zooey, whose eyes were about to pop out. "Talk to the other seventh graders — find out what they want."

Zooey raised her hand.

"Yes?" Lily said.

"Do I have the floor now?" Zooey said.

"You do," Lily said. This was fun. She started to un-deflate.

"If we ask kids, aren't they gonna say stuff like, 'We want Domino's Pizza for lunch' or 'We want a longer summer vacation'?" Zooey said.

"Sure," Ian said. "But some people might actually have some real ideas."

Lily found herself staring at Ian. He hadn't said one dumb thing since they'd started the meeting. He hadn't even punched Lee on the arm or burped out loud.

"Does somebody want to move that?" she said.

She saw Ms. Ferringer stifle a giggle, but that was okay. Lily was on a roll.

"I so move," Ian said.

"Will anybody second?" Lily said.

The motion passed, and Lily told everyone to start polling right away.

Mr. Chester, their math teacher, was absent fifth period, and the substitute gave them a study hall. Lily took full advantage of the opportunity to do interviews.

Every person told her almost the same thing.

"I hate fund-raisers. Everybody in my neighborhood hides when they see me coming because I'm always selling something."

"This school stinks. I hate coming here."

"Who even worries about grades anymore — even in the accelerated classes?"

Lily had all of that running around in her head when she got to her locker after school that day. When Ian stepped up beside her, she didn't see him at first, and when she did, she jumped, knocking her geography book out of the locker and onto her foot. She waited for him to say she was a klutz. But he just leaned over and picked it up.

"You okay?" he said.

She nodded, too surprised to speak.

"I just wanted to say, I think we're gonna make a great team," he said.

"You do?" Lily said.

"Don't you?" Ian cocked one eyebrow up over his glasses frame.

"Oh, yeah, for sure!" Lily said. Her voice never stayed lost for long. "I've already done a bunch of polling, and everybody's way fed up with this place."

"Same here. And I think we can change some of that. You're a good president."

Then Ian smiled and walked away. Lily watched him until she couldn't see him anymore.

This is gonna be so cool, she thought when he'd disappeared. *I have to get Mom and Dad to let me do this. I have to!*

Chapter 3

That night after supper, Mom and Dad sat down with Lily in the family room. Joe and Art had been asked to leave them alone, which made Lily's palms go clammy. When her parents cleared the room, they usually meant business.

But Lily had her own agenda, and she started right off with it.

"This isn't just another one of my new hobbies," she said the minute she hit the couch. "I know I haven't been very mature about my interests in the past, but this is different. I'm going to be very responsible about this, because me and the other officers — I mean, the other officers and me — are gonna really try to make a difference where it counts. What I really need from you guys is some help with those rule things for running a meeting. I already know it's what I'm supposed to be doing."

She took a big breath. Trying to sound as grown-up as Ian did was definitely hard.

"It's 'the other officers and I'," Dad said. "And I appreciate your seriousness about this." He stopped to take off his glasses and nibble a little on the earpiece. "But you still have an awful lot on your plate for a twelve-year-old girl."

Lily could feel her heart sinking. "Do you mean I have to give up being president? Even though I'm just getting started?"

"We're not robots, Lil," Mom said. "We're considering your feelings."

"Here's the plan," Dad said. He put his glasses on the table. Lily knew that five minutes later he'd be wondering where he put them. But his eyes weren't vague the way they often were. He focused them right on Lily — not necessarily a good sign. "Your mother and I want you to pray about all the things you're involved in and see if you can determine what things God really seems to want you to spend your time on."

"I've already done that," Lily said. "God says yes."

"Really?" Mom said. "How do you know?"

Lily shrugged. "It just feels right," she said.

Mom and Dad gave each other one of those I-know-what-you're-thinking looks.

"Feelings are definitely important," Dad said. He patted his pocket and then looked fuzzily around him. Lily picked up his glasses and handed them to him. "Feelings are important," he said, as he polished the glasses on the sleeve of his sweater, "but they aren't always our best indicator of God's will. The Lord gave you a brain, and it seems to me that's what you need to use in this situation."

"But I've thought about it!" Lily said.

"Have you thought about your spiritual gifts and whether you're using those for God?" Dad said.

Lily blinked at him. "What spiritual gifts? You mean like my lily cross Mudda gave me?" She fingered the cross from her grandmother that hung from a chain around her neck.

"Not that kind of gift, Lil," Mom said. "God's given everybody at least one gift that can be used to serve God's community. You know how some people are really great Sunday school teachers — "

"And some aren't," Lily put in.

"Exactly," Dad said. "You need to find out if leadership is a gift you have, or whether you ought to put your energies where your real gifts are."

"How am I gonna find out if I have a leadership gift if I don't try it?" Lily said.

Her parents looked at each other again. Dad even put on his glasses and squinted through the lenses, his eyes as blue and intense as Lily knew hers were at the moment.

"Let's do this," he said finally. "You continue to discuss this with God in your prayers, and in the meantime go ahead and be class president —"

"Yes!" Lily said. "Thank you!"

Dad put his hand up, and Lily clapped hers over her mouth. "But — if it appears at any time that this is not something you should do — that it isn't the best use of your gifts — you'll do the right thing and resign."

"And meanwhile," Mom said, "we will expect you to keep your grades up and do your chores and keep your quiet time."

Lily was bobbing her head with every item, but Dad said, "Maybe we ought to write all of this down in a contract. What have I done with my glasses?"

Mom's mouth twitched. "You're wearing them, hon," she said.

Lily posted the contract on her bulletin board in her room, and after she'd done her homework — and read from the book Dad had given her before she'd come upstairs, called *Robert's Rules of Order* — she started right in, writing to God about the gift of leadership and how she was sure she had it and how she was going to use it. That naturally led to thoughts about changing school rules — and before she'd written half a page she was convinced she was already doing what God wanted her to do.

The only problem right now was that it was hard to concentrate. From Art's attic room right above her, music was blaring out of Art's stereo and rattling her overhead light fixture.

"So much for quiet time," Lily said to Otto.

Sighing, she padded her way barefoot out of her room and up the stairs, where she had to beat on Art's door with her fist before he heard her.

"Enter!" he called out over the noise.

Lily pushed the door open and shoved her head in. "Could you turn that down?!" she shouted.

Art looked up from his computer, cupped his hand to his ear, and said, "What?"

Lily marched over to the stereo to give the volume dial a twist.

"Step away from the amplifier," Art said, his voice loud and heavy like somebody on *Law and Order* making an arrest. "Put your hands up and step away."

"Then *you* turn it down!" Lily shouted.

Art nudged the volume down a couple of decibels with the tip of his finger. "What's the problem?" he said.

"I'm trying to concentrate on important stuff down there, and I can't with this thing blaring," Lily said.

"And I'm trying to concentrate on important stuff up *here*, and I can't with*out* this thing blaring." Art propped his feet on the desk. "Music soothes the soul of the savage beast."

"Oh," Lily said. "It does?"

"As you will find out when you enter true adolescence and discover that schoolwork can be done only if you have your tunes playing at least three notches above what your parents can stand." Art grinned slyly. "Why do you think they gave me the attic room?"

"How do you concentrate in school, then?" Lily said. "*Our* teachers make us do everything in, like, total silence."

"Ah, the vacuum approach," Art said. "Yeah, it's pretty much like that in high school too. My theory is that if they'd play music—real music, not the elevator variety—in the halls between classes and in the cafeteria, achievement would skyrocket."

"Huh," Lily said. The wheels were already turning in her head.

"Like that's ever gonna happen," Art said. "In the first place, it would be the administrators who would pick the stuff, and with my luck we'd get stuck with Lawrence Welk. No — Yanni. No — worse — Barry Manilow — "

Art was starting to look a little green, but Lily could feel herself tingling.

"Thanks, Art," she said as she turned toward the door.

"For what?" he said.

"For the idea."

Lily went straight to the bench the next morning so she'd be sure to catch Deputy Dog when she strolled by. Since she didn't appear to be tracking anybody down at the moment, Lily said, "Could I ask you a question?"

"Sure." Deputy Dog propped her foot up on the bench and leaned on her knee.

"Is there any school-board rule against having music at school," Lily said, "you know, like in the cafeteria during lunch?"

Deputy Dog cocked her squarish head to one side and squinted for a moment while Lily waited, holding her breath.

"No, I don't think so," she said. "That would be up to the individual school."

Lily nodded in a businesslike way and said, "Thank you. That's all I needed."

Deputy Dog nodded and, putting her thumbs in her belt, took the steps two at a time in the direction of some kind of middle-school ruckus. Lily dove for her backpack and a pencil and paper, but Suzy arrived just then, which was even better.

"Start making a list, Suzy," Lily said instead of "hi." "Call it 'Ideas for Change.' Number one is gonna be — music in the cafeteria."

As Suzy wrote down everything exactly as Lily said it — with Lily looking over her shoulder — Zooey arrived and immediately dug a Polaroid camera out of her backpack and snapped a couple of pictures for the scrapbook. Lily was beaming. Did this feel like God or what?

As soon as she was sure Suzy had the whole thing down and Zooey had gotten it on film from every possible angle, Lily remembered that she hadn't told Ian her idea yet.

"I wish I knew where Ian was first period," she said out loud.

"Computers," Suzy said.

Lily stared at her. "How did you know that?"

"I got everybody's schedules so you'd always know where to find us."

"Wow," Lily said. "I think you've got one of the God gifts, Suze. I don't know what it's called, but I'm sure you've got it."

"Suzy has gift?" Kresha said as she arrived, breathless and sparkly-eyed.

"I'll explain later — at Girlz today," Lily said. "I have to go do officer stuff."

She was sure some of the sparkle went out of Kresha's eyes, and as she turned to head for the computer room, Lily made a vow to give Kresha some kind of assignment.

I know! she thought. *I'll find out what her gift is and give her something that matches it!*

She started up the steps and looked down, hopefully to catch Kresha's eye and smile at her. Just as she did, Reni passed the bench with Monique beside her. This time, Reni didn't even turn when Kresha called out to her. She seemed to be attached to every word that was coming out of Monique's mouth. She was nodding so hard all her beaded braids were bouncing.

Lily felt a pang. It was one thing for Reni and her to be involved in different things, but to be friends with different people was something Lily wasn't sure she liked.

I'll write her a Girlz Gram, she decided as she hurried up the stairs. But it would have to be later. Right now, she had class business to take care of.

Ian was in the computer room when she got there, tapping away at the keyboard, eyes glued to the screen. When Lily whispered "hi," he turned around, gave her a grin, and said, "What's up?"

When Lily told him her idea, his eyes lit up behind his glasses. "Cool!" he said. "And Deputy Dog told you it was up to the school — like the principal?"

Lily nodded happily. The only thing better than getting an incredibly brilliant idea was having somebody else think it was incredibly brilliant too.

"Have you told everybody else?" he said.

"Everybody except Lee," Lily said. "Oh — and Ms. Ferringer."

"You think we oughta have a meeting right away — like at lunch?"

"Definitely," Lily said. "I'll tell Suzy and Zooey — you tell Lee."

"What about Ms. Ferringer?"

They gave each other a look. Lily wasn't sure, but she thought it was probably an I-know-what-you're-thinking look.

During second period, Lily had some time to jot down more ideas for the meeting. But there wasn't any time to think about it in third period because Mrs. Reinhold gave a vocabulary test.

As usual, Lily was one of the first ones finished, but she didn't look around the room the way she did in Ms. Ferringer's class. Mrs. Reinhold wouldn't have taken her eyes off of the class if she'd lost her entire car. Lily had to be content with staring at the back of Ashley's blonde head. That wasn't usually her favorite view, but this time it made Lily think about Ashley nominating her.

I know she did it to be sure Benjamin would be elected, Lily thought. *But if it hadn't been for her, I'd never have gotten this chance.* Lily nibbled on a fingernail. *Should I thank her?* That seemed like a thing a leader would do.

Mrs. Reinhold called time and told them to exchange papers for grading. Ashley barely looked at Lily as she tossed her paper onto Lily's desk and snatched Lily's out of her hand. That made it harder, but when they were finished correcting, Lily scribbled a note on a scrap of paper and passed it to Ashley with her quiz.

Thanks for nominating me, it said. *I'm going to try to do a good job. Is there anything around here that you want to see changed?*

That got Ashley to turn and give Lily a long, curled-lip look. Then she whipped back around and began to scribble on the back of the note. When Mrs. Reinhold told them to pass the papers forward, Ashley flipped the note to her.

Yeah, it said. *You can get us more parties—and you can change my answer to number 5.*

Even as the kid behind her was poking the row's papers into Lily's back, she could only sit there, stunned.

She couldn't be asking me to cheat, Lily thought. Ashley was smart enough to be in accelerated classes, so she didn't need to cheat to make good grades.

No way, she thought. *Ashley's just kidding.*

As she stuck the papers in Ashley's hand, Lily gathered up a laugh and delivered it. "You're funny, Ashley," she said.

Ashley gave her another curled lip and flipped herself back around.

Chapter 4

At lunch, the five officers bent their heads together, and while Suzy wrote everything down word for word, they came up with a proposal to present to the principal, Mr. Tanini. Lily tingled through the process, especially when she had a chance to use her copy of *Robert's Rules of Order.* She thought she'd probably tingle right out of her skin if this thing got any better.

The way they set it up, there would be music playing between classes in the halls and in the cafeteria during lunch. Kids could turn in their CDs with certain songs requested so everybody would have a chance to hear their kind of music.

"When can we take this to the office?" Lily said to Ms. Ferringer.

Through the whole process, Ms. Ferringer had been sitting quietly in her chair, curling a strand of hair around her finger. Now she smiled as if she were about to explain something to a first grade reading group.

"Like I told you before," she said, "I appreciate your enthusiasm, but you really don't have to do all this."

"We know we don't *have* to," Lily said. "We *want* to."

"That's right," Ian said, giving Lily one of his grins. "Too many people do just as much as they have to. We want to go the extra mile."

Lily was impressed and made a silent vow to work a little on her vocabulary.

Mr. Ferringer looked more amused than impressed. She squeezed Ian's hand and said, "Okay. Why don't you let me correct the punctuation and have Suzy type it up. I'll log her onto my computer in here. I think I can trust you to use it for officer business."

"You can *so* trust her!" Lily said. "She has the gift of — dependableness."

Ms. Ferringer laughed a deep, raspy chuckle. "You crack me up, Lily," she said.

When she and Suzy had gone to the side of the room where Ms. Ferringer had her computer, Lily looked at Ian. "I was being serious," she said.

"At least she's in a better mood today," Zooey whispered.

Lee nodded toward Ms. Ferringer's desk. Lily was quickly figuring out that Lee didn't talk much in words. He mostly used head jerks to get his point across. She followed his nod to the desk. Ms. Ferringer's keys were there.

"There's your reason," Ian said. Then he and Lily grinned at each other.

While Suzy was typing the proposal, Lily reported her other findings. "Kids want, like, parties," she said. She didn't add that at least one of them also wanted free answers.

Zooey's gray eyes widened. "Could we really do that?" she said.

Lee gave his head-jerk of approval.

Ms. Ferringer rejoined them, looking like it was all she could do not to burst out laughing. "Let's see how we do with this project first," she said.

Lily's eyes at once connected with Ian's. *We're gonna do great with this project,* his said. Hers agreed.

Suzy was finished before the end of lunch period, and Lily and Ian led the way to the office, the perfectly typed proposal in Lily's hand.

She had visions of being ushered into Mr. Tanini's office and placing the proposal into his hands and then watching him grow more and more impressed as he read it. But the secretary told them he was in the cafeteria, and they could leave it with her. Ian gave Lily a nudge.

"We can give it to him ourselves," he said into her ear.

Lily pulled the paper back from the secretary's outstretched hand. "This is urgent," Lily said. "We'll deliver it."

Feeling her most leaderlike yet, Lily led her parade of officers to the cafeteria, where a brief search located tall, bald Mr. Tanini in the vicinity of Ashley's table.

As Lily and company marched toward him, heads came up from plates of Tater Tots and cans of soda on all sides. Lily just homed in on Mr. Tanini.

"Just remember what I told you," he was saying to Ashley, Chelsea, Bernadette, and Benjamin when Lily stopped beside him. "Hold the noise down over here."

"Mr. Tanini?" Lily said. "I think we have something that will soothe the soul of these savage beasts."

Out of the corner of her eye, Lily could see Ian looking impressed. Once in a while, having Art as a brother came in handy.

"Do you, now?" Mr. Tanini said.

"Right here," Lily said, and presented him with the paper.

He studied Lily closely and then let his eyes scan over Zooey, Suzy, Lee, and Ian. "Our new seventh-grade class officers," he said. "You have your fund-raising idea already? You guys are really on the ball."

"That isn't *exactly* what it is," Ian said. "We thought this might be better."

"We want to make a difference!" Zooey said.

Zooey was getting into it. Lily made a mental note to figure out Zooey's gift.

"I see," Mr. Tanini said. "Do you want to give me an idea what this is about?"

"Lily can tell you," Ian said. "It's her baby."

Mr. Tanini's eyes twinkled at Lily. "All right," he said. "Fill me in."

Lily took a huge breath and poured out the ideas in the proposal, being careful not to use too many "gonnas" and "likes" and to get at least one big word in there. When she was finished, Ian was grinning, and Mr. Tanini was nodding.

"Let me look it over," he said. "I'll have an answer to you by the end of the day."

Lily was only briefly disappointed that he didn't give them an enthusiastic yes on the spot, and after handshakes all around, started by Ian, she was feeling positive again as she turned to lead the way out. Then she stopped so abruptly, Ian nearly ran up the back of her leg.

At the end of the table where the Girlz always ate sat Kresha. Alone.

Lily abandoned the officers and went over to her. "Where's Reni?" she said.

"She practicing," Kresha said. She seemed to be trying to look cheerful, but Lily could see how lonely her eyes were. She wasn't sure what to do.

"Come on, Lily," Suzy said as she came up to her. "We better go —" She stopped, her eyes drooping as she saw Kresha. "Did you eat by yourself?" she said.

Kresha nodded and attempted a smile.

"That's brave!" Zooey said. "I'd be afraid people would think nobody wanted to be with me."

Lily winced, and she could feel Suzy poking Zooey. Being careful about people's feelings definitely wasn't one of Zooey's gifts.

"We'll see you sixth period," Lily said. "You want to be my lab partner today?"

Kresha brightened and nodded eagerly, but Lily still felt bad as she hurried off.

Ian was waiting for Lily at the door. "Hey," he said, "you want to have everybody meet in Ms. F's room after school, and we'll wait there for Mr. Tanini's answer?"

"Sure," Lily said. "I'll tell Suzy and Zooey."

"Sweet," Ian said.

"What about the Girlz Only meeting?" Suzy said when Lily told them.

"My mom made cheese balls for us," Zooey said.

Lily twisted her lips for a minute. There had to be a way to fit it all in. Finally, she said, "This won't take that long—probably just a couple minutes after school's out. Then we can go to Girlz Only." She glanced at her watch. "I'll catch you guys later."

She was out of breath by the time she grabbed her backpack, told Ms. Ferringer about the meeting, and dashed off to math. But it felt good to be busy and important.

The feeling continued that afternoon after sixth period when they regrouped in Ms. F's room. Lily was so jazzed that she suggested they brainstorm for more ideas while they waited. Suzy got out her notebook, but Ian said, "We oughta skip a step and just have you type things while we're talking. Could we use the computer, Ms. F.?"

"You guys are really on a roll," she said. She was giving them the aren't-you-cute grin, but she went to the computer and logged on. Before she'd even returned to her desk, the ideas were flowing, and Suzy had a whole screen filled up when the door opened and a shiny bald head appeared. Lily felt her heart skip several beats.

"Anybody home?" Mr. Tanini said. "Looks like *everybody's* home! You sure have an enthusiastic group here, Ms. Ferringer."

"Don't I, though?" she said. For the first time, she didn't look as if the kindergarten class had just performed "The Itsy Bitsy Spider." She looked proud.

"Would you like to know my response to your proposal?" Mr. Tanini said.

Yes! Lily wanted to squeal. But she tried to look executive and said, "Would you like to sit down?"

Lee dragged another chair over, and Ian stood up until Mr. Tanini sat down. Lily was liking this formal thing more and more. She made a vow to wear a skirt the next day. Right now she riveted her attention on Mr. Tanini.

"First, let me say I'm impressed with your professionalism," he said.

"Thank you, sir," Ian said.

"Yes, thank you," Lily chimed in.

"And I've decided to approve at least part of your proposal. I will agree to music in the cafeteria during lunch on Fridays with these conditions. You must form a committee, with Ms. Ferringer advising it, to get acquainted with the sound equipment in the office, so you can broadcast the music over the intercom, and choose the music from the things the students bring in." He glanced at Ms. Ferringer, who was twisting a lock of her hair. "I'm sure you know what kind of music would be appropriate," he said.

"Yes!" she said. She let go of the curl as if she'd been caught picking her nose.

"All right, then," Mr. Tanini said. "I'm anxious to see how this pans out."

"Thank you, sir," Lily said.

Actually, she was ready to dance around the room, and she was waiting for Mr. Tanini to get out the door first. But when he opened it, he said, "Can I help you?"

"Yes, sir," a familiar voice said. "We're looking for Lily Robbins and — "

"You're in luck," Mr. Tanini said, as he stepped aside to reveal Reni, Kresha, and Zooey's mother.

They all looked hopping mad.

Chapter 5

Lily could feel herself sinking down in her seat.

"Didn't you tell them we were gonna be late?" she whispered to Zooey.

"No!" Zooey whispered back. "I thought Suzy was gonna do it."

"It was at *your* house," Suzy hissed. "I thought *you* did it!"

"Lily's the leader!" Zooey said. "She shoulda done it!"

"We gotta go," Lily said to Ian and Lee, who were watching curiously as the Girlz hissed at each other like a trio of snakes.

Suzy already had her backpack on and was headed for the door. Zooey, on the other hand, was shrinking down in her desk as if she hoped her mother wouldn't see her.

"Zooey," Mrs. Hoffman said.

So much for that. Lily hurried past her, muttering, "I'm sorry." Behind her, she heard Mrs. Hoffman say, "I even made cheese balls, Zooey."

It wasn't much more pleasant out in the hall. Kresha was scowling in the face of Suzy's apology, and Reni was glaring at Lily, hands on hips.

"I'm *so* sorry," Lily said. "This came up at the last minute and I thought—"

"You thought we'd just wait for you," Reni said. Her brown eyes were snapping, and she was doing that E.T. thing with her neck. Yeah, she was mad. "Admit it," Reni said. "You ditched us so you could go do your latest thing."

"This isn't just some thing!" Lily said. "This is my gift!"

"Yeah — until the next gift or whatever it is comes along. You never stick to anything, but you expect the rest of us to be around when you're done."

You should talk! Lily wanted to say. *You ditch us all the time so you can go play the violin — you even let Kresha eat all by herself.* Lily sniffed. *At least I don't take up with other people while I'm doing it the way you're doing with Monique —*

Lily opened her mouth, but Ian stepped out into the hall, and Lily didn't want to spout off in front of him. But what was she supposed to do? She'd told Mom and Dad she could do it all. She thought *God* said so —

And then inspiration struck. Lily grabbed Reni by the arm.

"I want you to be head of a committee," Lily said.

Reni narrowed her eyes. "What committee?"

Quickly Lily told her about the music proposal and how they needed somebody to be sure it all happened.

"Who in the whole seventh grade knows more about music than you?" Lily said. "If you're chairman of my committee, we can work together."

The minute it was out of her mouth, Lily saw the teary look on Kresha's face.

Reni must have seen it too, because she said, "I'll do it on one condition: Kresha's the rest of the committee. She works with me."

"Yes!" Lily said. "I was gonna suggest that!"

"What is 'committee'?" Kresha said. Her eyes were already hopeful.

The explanation was going to have to wait, however, because Zooey and her mom came out then, and although Mrs. Hoffman said she would take everyone home, she was stiff and cold all the way to the van and during the ride as she dropped off each of the Girlz.

"Why's she so mad?" Lily whispered to Suzy.

"Well, it *is* 5:30 already," Suzy whispered back.

"Uh-oh," Lily said.

That was an understatement. When Lily walked in her front door, she could hear her mother clattering silverware in the kitchen, doing Lily's table setting chore. Lily dumped her backpack and sprang to the kitchen wearing a giant smile.

"Hi, Mom!" she said. "Sorry I'm late! Time got away from me — "

Mom shot her a look that wiped off her grin. "I called Zooey's, but there was no answer. Weren't you supposed to be at her house after school?"

Lily grabbed some napkins and started folding. "I had class officer stuff after school, and it ran long. We didn't make it to Zooey's. But we did get our first proposal passed."

"Before you start celebrating," Mom said, "I want you to remember that you made some serious promises about your chores and your other responsibilities."

"I know," Lily said. She focused on the careful refolding of a paper napkin, which was by now starting to look like origami. "It won't happen again."

"Can you really say that?"

Lily looked up quickly. Mom had her arms folded. Her eyes were serious.

"Just remember that you're supposed to be asking God what's really important," Mom said.

"Oh, I do," Lily said.

Mom turned to the microwave, which was beeping insistently. Lily added, "I'll keep praying about it."

She was doing that later in the evening in her room with Otto when Joe pounded on the door and said, "You got a phone call." Then he snickered and added, "It's a boy."

He's lying, of course, Lily thought. *Boys don't call me.* Joe was a pain.

She sighed, climbed off her bed, and opened the door. Joe pretended the sight of her was so horrible he had to jump back and cover his eyes.

"You sure you want to talk to her?" he said into the phone. "She's pretty scary."

Lily snatched the phone out of his hand and slammed the door in his face.

"Hello?" she said into the receiver.

"Lily?" It was Ian.

Lily wanted to crawl under the bed — right after she bonked Joe over the head.

"Yeah," she said. "Hi, Ian."

"Was that your kid brother?" he said.

"Yes. Unfortunately."

"I got one too. Mine belches into the phone every time somebody calls me."

"Gross," Lily said.

She grinned, and she could feel Ian grinning back. She shoved Otto aside and curled up on her bed.

"Hey," Ian said, "we didn't get to finish our idea list today. You want to meet before school in Ms. Ferringer's room?"

"Sure," Lily said. "What time?"

"Seven thirty?"

Lily did a quick calculation. The Girlz usually met at 7:45, and first period started at 8:00. "How long do you think it'll take?" she said.

"Ten — fifteen minutes?"

"Okay — I'll be there."

But just to be sure she didn't let the Girlz down again, she got to school at 7:25 the next morning. If she and Ian got an early start, she could still meet with them.

Ian wasn't there yet when she went into Ms. Ferringer's room—but Ashley and Benjamin were. As Lily closed the door behind her, their heads popped up from Ms. Ferringer's computer.

"Oh," Lily said. "I didn't know anybody would be using it."

They looked at her blankly, then exchanged glances with each other, and scrambled for their backpacks. They were out the door before Lily even got hers off. She was still trying to figure it all out a few minutes later when Ian arrived.

"Dude," he said. "Ashley and Benjamin about ran me down in the hall."

"They did the same thing to me when they left here," Lily said.

"So—you ready? I got some more great ideas."

"Cool," Lily said.

Ian nodded at the computer, Lee-style. "You think Ms. Ferringer would mind if we used her computer?"

"Probably not," Lily said. "Ashley and Benjamin were using it when I got here."

"Cool beans," Ian said, and headed for it. But after he'd sat down and clicked the mouse a couple of times, he shook his head. "You have to have a password to even get on," he said. "That's weird. I guess Ms. Ferringer got those guys on before she went out."

Lily shrugged. "We can just write stuff down and Suzy can type it later."

They were hard at work on their list a few minutes later when Ms. Ferringer breezed in, eyes blinking furiously in her contact lenses. She stopped in the doorway when they looked up and seemed even more confused than usual.

"Well, hi," she said. "Who let you guys in?"

"Nobody," Lily said. "The door was unlocked. Isn't it okay for us to be here?"

"It's fine," Ms. Ferringer said. "It's strange, that's all."

She continued to mutter to herself as she went to her desk, and then she looked up again as if she'd just remembered they were there. "I just saw Mr. Tanini. He says he'll need an announcement to read over the intercom this afternoon about the music thing. I was going to write it, but since you guys are here — "

"Gotcha," Ian said.

He looked at Lily, who pulled out a fresh sheet of paper.

In five minutes they had it done and approved by Ms. Ferringer and were on their way to the office with it. Lily was surprised when the warning bell rang as they'd dropped it off.

"Is it that late already?" she said.

"Yeah. Time flies when you're having fun," Ian said. Then he grinned at her.

He's right, Lily thought. *It really is fun.* That feeling kept her floating through first and second periods. She hit the ground in third when Reni managed to slip her a Girlz Gram in spite of Mrs. Reinhold's watchful eye.

You ditched everybody again this morning, it said. *I even came — but you didn't.*

Lily sneaked a glance at her. Reni immediately looked up from her *Adventures in Literature* book, as if she'd been waiting.

I'm sorry, Lily said with her eyes.

Are you really? Reni said with hers.

After class, to Lily's surprise, Reni waited for her in the hall. Lily launched right in with promises.

"No more working on officer business in the morning or after school," she said.

"Huh," Reni said.

"You're not exactly around all the time either, you know," Lily said.

"I'm practicing — and I let everybody know that. We never know where you are."

And we never know who you're with, Lily wanted to say. But she swallowed that urge. She was a leader. She had to stay positive.

"It'll be different from now on," she said instead. "And now that you're head of a committee, we'll be together more."

"Sure," Reni said.

They walked along in silence for a minute. Then Reni said, "What country did you draw for that geography thing?"

"France," Lily said.

"I got the Galapagos Islands. I don't even know where that is."

It felt like a truce — sort of — and Lily let it be. It was better than having Reni not speak to her.

It'll get better once she sees how important my leadership work is, Lily assured herself.

When the bell rang in geography class, Ms. Ferringer stood up with a rat's nest of papers in her hand.

"Those are our tests," Reni whispered.

Lily nodded. She hoped hers was on top. Ms. Ferringer always passed the papers back in order of grade from highest to lowest. Lily always wanted A's, but especially now when Mom and Dad were watching everything like they had her under investigation.

"Ashley?" Ms. Ferringer said, and put Ashley's paper in front of her. "Benjamin — Chelsea — Bernadette."

Lily was starting to feel queasy. Reni poked Lily.

"Since when did they start studying?" she whispered.

Lily shrugged. If the ABCs had gotten better scores than she did, she might be in trouble.

But the paper that appeared on her desk was marked 97/A. Lily felt herself practically melting into a puddle.

"Yikes," Reni whispered. "Ashley and them musta gotten hundreds."

"Yeah," Lily said. What had suddenly motivated them to work hard at anything but flirting with each other?

45

"All right," Ms. Ferringer said. "Get to work on your projects."

Lily dug out what she'd been able to find in Dad's study on France the night before. As things began to settle down, it became obvious that the ABCs had no intention of getting down to work anytime soon. Ms. Ferringer, however, didn't seem to notice. She was already becoming flush-faced because three people were asking her questions at the same time.

"Hey, Lily," somebody said at her elbow. "You wanna work in the library?"

It was Ian, grinning down at her. He glanced toward the ABCs. "Who can work in here?" he said.

"Yeah," Lily said.

He went to get them passes, and Reni poked Lily in the back.

"You're going to the library with *him*?" she said.

"Well—yeah," Lily said.

"Huh," Reni said. She propped up the G volume of the encyclopedia in front of her on the desktop.

"What?" Lily said.

"Nothing," Reni said.

"Ready?" Ian said.

He grinned. Reni didn't. Lily followed him out of the room.

Chapter
6

On the way to the library, Ian chattered away while Lily half-listened. She couldn't forget the stony look on Reni's face as she was leaving.

What's happening with her? Lily thought, while she nodded and smiled at Ian. *We've been best friends for, like, ever. Now it seems like all we do is fight.*

She gave Ian another nod — and then she realized he'd asked her a question.

"What?" she said.

"I said are you going as nuts as I am?"

She blinked.

"About our announcement this afternoon," he said. "We've only been talking about it for the last five minutes!"

"Oh — yeah," Lily said. "I'm going nuts about a lot of things. Sometimes it's hard to tell which one I'm flipping out over right now."

"You're pretty cool," Ian said, and opened the library door for her.

From that point on, until sixth period, the announcement about the music-in-the-cafeteria program took up all her thoughts. When the end of sixth period finally came and Mr. Tanini cleared his throat over the intercom, it was all Lily could do not to shush everybody around her in science class.

That didn't turn out to be necessary anyway. As soon as Mr. Tanini read, "This Friday, the cafeteria will start rocking with the tunes of your choice," everybody in the room started shushing each other.

"If you have a request for a song you want to hear during lunch on a Friday, bring your tape or CD, clearly labeled with your name and the song you want played over the intercom, and place it in the slot of the locked box on the front counter in the office. All requests will be reviewed by a committee, so no foul language or suggestive lyrics, please. This project is being sponsored by the seventh-grade class."

There were other announcements, but Lily was sure nobody heard them, because the whole room came alive with conversation.

"Is this for real? We can listen to *our* music?"

"Nah — you know they're gonna stick Neil Diamond or somebody in there."

"Who's Neil Diamond?"

"I think this sounds cool."

Lily felt herself grinning from one gold loop earring to the other — ones she'd borrowed from Mom because they looked more professional than Lily's usual pink plastic balls or orange dangles. The other kids probably hadn't appreciated the work she and Ian had put into parts like, "No foul language or suggestive lyrics, please," but they'd definitely gotten the idea that this was a huge deal. After school at the lockers, she was bombarded with questions.

"Man, whose idea was that?"

"Does it really mean no elevator music? It isn't gonna be oldies, is it?"

"How'd you ever talk Tanini into it?"

It's all about leadership, Lily wanted to tell them. But she smiled and said thank you and answered questions—and felt like she could have led just about anything.

The only person who seemed concerned was Ms. Ferringer. In fourth period the next day, she called Lily and Ian out into the hall.

"This music thing is starting tomorrow?" she said. "Isn't that a little soon?"

Ian and Lily looked at each other.

"That's what we wrote on the announcement," Lily said.

"The one we had you approve before we turned it in," Ian said.

Ms. Ferringer blinked, sending her contacts swimming around in her eyes. "I guess I missed that," she said. "You sure you can pull this together by then? I mean, if it bombs, you guys aren't the only ones who are going to look like you don't know what you're doing."

"Reni and Kresha are very responsible," Lily said.

"But we'll check in with them today," Ian said. "Just to make you feel better."

The way he nodded reassuringly at Ms. Ferringer, it seemed to Lily like he was the teacher and she was the kid. Ms. Ferringer seemed to feel a little better as she shooed them back into the room.

"Do you know where Reni and Kresha hang out at lunch?" Ian asked. "Reni went to the library, or we could talk to her now."

"Yeah," Lily said, "I know where they'll be. We can—" She paused to find just the right professional-sounding word. "We can consult with them there."

Reni stayed in the library all period, so Lily didn't have a chance to tell her about the meeting. Kresha was at the usual spot at the Girlz table with Suzy and Zooey, but Reni was not available for consultation.

"Where is she?" Lily said.

"Her and that Monique girl came in and bought their lunches and took them back to the orchestra room," Zooey said.

Lily felt another jealous pang.

"We can just consult with Kresha," Ian said to Lily.

"What's 'consult'?" Zooey said. "Does that mean we gotta leave you alone?"

"We just want to check in with Kresha and see how the music committee is doing," Lily said.

She turned to Kresha and for the first time noticed that she was staring at her half-eaten baloney sandwich, shoulders sloped as if she were trying to disappear.

"You okay, Kresh?" Lily said, sinking onto the bench beside her.

Kresha's head said yes, but the rest of her body looked as if she wanted to climb in with the baloney.

"What's wrong?" Lily said. "Has somebody been teasing you again?"

"No," Kresha said. "I am fine."

Lily was sure she wasn't telling the truth, but she knew Kresha could be pretty stubborn. She glanced uneasily at Ian, who sat down across from Kresha, hands folded. He looked so official that Lily folded hers too.

"We just wanted to check in with you," Ian said. "Is everything going okay so far? You've got the sound system all checked out for tomorrow?"

Kresha hesitated before she nodded.

"Is something the matter with it?" Lily said.

"Oh, no!" Kresha's head popped up, and she swatted her bangs out of her eyes. "Everything fine! We got some music today in box. We be ready for tomorrow."

"When are you and Reni gonna sit down and choose the songs?" Ian said.

Kresha studied her sandwich again. "Today," she said.

"When today?" Ian said.

"I do not know," Kresha said, still watching the mayonnaise squish out as she squeezed her bread.

Ian gave Lily a concerned look, but Lily was more worried about Kresha. It wasn't like her to hide behind her lunch. Still — if this project flopped —

No — she had to be a leader. She had to be positive — hand out plenty of praise. Lily sat up straighter and patted Kresha on the back.

"They'll get it done," she said. "I have confidence in them."

Kresha gave her a sideways glance and half of a smile. Lily walked away with Ian feeling very much the leader. There was no doubt Mom and Dad were going to agree.

A glimmer of a thought — that she was supposed to be praying about it — flashed through her brain, but she let it flash back out. She'd check it out with God tonight.

God didn't seem to have a different opinion about it that night, and the next day, Friday, Lily was convinced she and God were thinking alike.

She put on the gray wool skirt she usually only wore to church with a navy blazer and a white turtleneck. She begged Mom to let her wear some of her pantyhose. But when Mom said she had enough trouble keeping them from getting runs when *she* was wearing them and that no, she couldn't borrow them, Lily settled for some gray tights and black loafers. It felt funny not to be wearing a sweatshirt and jeans to school, but she decided that was good, and she even put her hair in a bun — no easy feat with her mop of curls. She kept checking it in the rearview mirror of Dad's car to make sure it wasn't popping out in weird places the way Ms. Ferringer's did.

When lunchtime came, she, Ian, Lee, Zooey, and Suzy sat together at the Girlz table. Lily was so nervous she couldn't even take her peanut-butter-and-jelly sandwich out of its Baggie. She just nibbled anxiously on a potato chip until the first strains of music filtered through the cafeteria clatter. Almost like magic, people's voices lowered. One of the latest pop divas was soothing the savage beasts.

"It's working!" Lily whispered to Ian.

"Of course it is," he whispered back.

Not everybody liked it, but the instant the grumbling started from Shad Shifferdecker and his friends, the music switched to one of his top picks, and Shad's table changed *its* tune to "All right!" and "Now, *that's* what *I'm* talkin' about!"

At the Girlz table, there wasn't enough room on Lily's face for the smile she needed to show.

"They like it!" Zooey said, big eyes roaming the room in amazement.

Lee stuck up a thumb — and then he and Ian high-fived each other — and then their whole table high-fived. Lily wished she could run to the office, where Reni and Kresha were popping in CDs and pushing buttons, just to tell them how proud she was of them. She waited it out, though, so she could keep watching people's faces as their favorite songs came on. It was pleasant in the cafeteria for once. In fact, she didn't see even one corn dog sail through the air.

As soon as lunch was over, all of the officers raced to the office, where Kresha was putting scattered CDs back into their cases. Reni was watching her, arms folded across her chest, when Lily ran up to her.

"You guys were awesome!" Lily said. "It sounded just like the radio!"

"Everybody loved it!" Zooey said.

"I don't think anybody got mad," Suzy put in. "Not even the teachers."

"You like?" Kresha said.

"Yes!" Lily said, hugging her. "I think being a DJ's your gift."

Kresha grinned and tossed her bangs back. It was good to see her happy again.

But to Lily's surprise, Reni didn't look pleased. There wasn't a dimple within a hundred yards.

"Everything okay?" Lily murmured to her.

"No," Reni said. "Mr. Lamb's mad at me because I missed practice to do this."

"You already practice about a million times a day!" Lily said.

Reni rolled her eyes as if Lily had no idea what she was talking about. "Lunch is the only time I can practice with Monique," she said.

"Oh," Lily said. She knew the sting she felt inside was showing in her voice. "Well, it's only on Fridays. He can't even let you out for one day a week?"

"I don't know," Reni said.

"Do you want me to talk to him for you?" Lily said.

Reni's eyes scrunched up. "What good would that do?"

"Well, I *am* class president."

"Wow," Reni said.

"And you're so good at this, Reni. It's one of your gifts, and you ought to be using it."

"I have a gift for playing CDs? Whoopee." Reni sighed. "Okay," she said, "I'll talk to him."

Things went better between them for the rest of the day, and Lily was feeling pretty proud of the way she'd handled Reni.

You just have to be positive and lay on plenty of praise, she was telling herself as she headed for her locker after school. *How would I know that if it weren't exactly what God wanted me to be doing?*

She was so deep in thought that she had to try her locker combination twice to get the lock open. When somebody said, "Hey—Robbins," she jumped and dropped the lock on her foot. When she straightened from picking it up, Ashley was within a nose length.

"You're such a spastic," Ashley said. Then she stood there, curling her lip.

"So—did you want something?" Lily said, in her most patient-leader voice.

"Somebody told me that music in the cafeteria thing was your idea."

Here we go, Lily thought. *She's gonna tell me it was the geekiest thing on the planet.* But Lily straightened her shoulders and nodded. "Yeah," she said.

"Oh," Ashley said. "So you actually did something that wasn't totally lame."

It was about the closest Ashley had ever come to paying Lily a compliment. Lily savored it.

"Okay, so you lucked out," Ashley said. "But that's small-time. I bet you can't do something *really* big — not like we were gonna do if we'd gotten elected."

"Like what?" Lily said — staying calm and sophisticated. "We're always open."

Ashley's blue eyes took on a gleam as she put her hands on her hips. "All right," she said. "What about this. Can you get us a Christmas party the last day before vacation — *during* school?"

Are you kidding? Lily's thoughts screamed at her. *They're so not gonna let us have a party during school hours. We haven't done that since we left elementary!*

And right before Christmas? No way. The teachers were already talking about the memo they'd received about no parties and movies during the last week before vacation.

But Ashley was waiting, toe tapping. The gleam in her eyes was almost evil.

"I think we could get just about anything we wanted," Lily said. "It depends on whether we want it. I'll talk to the other officers and get back to you."

"Right," Ashley said. "Like that's really gonna happen."

"You said *you* guys were gonna — going to — try it. Why shouldn't we?"

"Because!" Ashley said, upper lip folding over itself. "You're not — us!"

She gave a high-pitched laugh that went up Lily's backbone as she flipped herself around and walked away.

No, Lily thought, *but we are us.*

Chapter

7

At Girlz Only that day, Zooey's mom's lips were pulled tight like a rubber band as she brought down a tray of warmed-up cheese balls. Lily made it a point to thank her about six times.

"Is your mom still mad at us?" Suzy said when Mrs. Hoffman was gone.

"She'll get over it," Zooey said, but she glanced at Lily.

"What?" Reni said. "What did your mom say about Lily, Zo?"

"I kinda forget," Zooey said.

"Well, kinda remember," Reni said. "We're not supposed to keep stuff from each other — at least that's the way it used to be."

"It still that way!" Kresha said.

"Huh," Reni said.

Suzy sat up uneasily on the yellow beanbag chair. "I'm sure she didn't say anything bad about Lily."

"Well, it was a little bit bad," Zooey said.

Lily was ready to explode out of her beanbag. "Would everybody stop talking about me like I'm not even here? For Pete's sake, Zooey — what did she say?"

"That you never stick to anything, and every time you start something new, it either gets us in trouble or hurts our feelings."

Suzy looked anxiously at Lily. "That doesn't hurt *your* feelings, does it?"

It wasn't hurt Lily was feeling. It was more the itchy sensation of not being understood. "It's okay," she said. "Zooey's mom just doesn't understand about gifts."

"Or maybe she does, but you keep switching gifts," Reni said.

"Reni!" Suzy said. "Lily's your best friend!"

"Does that mean I'm not supposed to tell her the truth?" Reni said.

"You mad at Lily?" Kresha said.

"Nope," Reni said. "Just saying it like it is."

The Girlz looked from Reni to Lily as if they were watching a Ping-Pong match.

"Look," Lily said, "I know everybody thinks I bounce all around, but I'm not doing that anymore. I've found my gift, which is leadership, so that's what I'm going to be into from now on—just like Zooey's got a gift for scrapbooking and Suzy's good at taking notes and typing stuff up and Reni and Kresha are, like, practically professional DJs." She put out both hands. "See? We all have our gifts."

Reni snorted out loud.

"What?" Lily said.

"Sure, we all have our gifts," Reni said. "Just as long as they fit in with what *you* wanna do. We're not Girlz Only anymore. We're Lily Only."

Suzy gulped. Zooey's eyes bulged. Kresha mumbled something in Croatian.

"That's *so* not true," Lily said.

"Yes, it is," Reni said—and then she popped two of the three balls she was juggling into her mouth and chewed. Lily could only stare.

"I don't see why we even meet anymore," Reni said with her mouth full. "We oughta just break up so you can go do whatever you want without having to drag us with you."

"But I *want* to drag you! I mean—I want to be with you guys."

"No, you don't. You just want us to follow you around." Reni abandoned the third cheese ball. Her eyes were flashing. "I'm pretty sick of it. I don't think I'm gonna come anymore. It's messing up my practice schedule anyway."

"Reni, no!" Zooey said. "It won't be any fun without you!"

Reni shrugged. She was watching Lily. So was everybody else.

"Why are you all looking at *me*?" Lily said. "What do you want me to do?"

"You're this big leader," Reni said. "You oughta know."

Then she collected her backpack and disappeared up the stairs.

By then, Suzy was crying, and Zooey was starting to sniffle.

"She coming back?" Kresha said.

"No!" Zooey wailed. "She's probably never coming back!"

"Girlz over then?" Kresha said.

Nobody answered. It was the silence that finally brought the tears to Lily's eyes.

When Lily got home, Mom and Dad were out, picking out carpet for the new addition, Art told her. Lily was relieved. She didn't want to tell them her leadership thing wasn't going so well at the moment.

She went into her room and flopped down on her bed. Otto crawled out from his under-the-bed hiding place to join her, but he sat up at the far corner of the mattress and surveyed her suspiciously from under his bushy, gray eyebrows.

"Good choice," Lily said. "I'm in a bad mood."

Otto lowered himself by his front paws, his eyes still on her.

"I *know* I'm a leader," she told him. She pointed to her bulletin board. "I'm following all the stuff on my contract. But people don't get it! The grown-ups laugh at me. Mom and Dad are making it way hard for me. And Reni — my best friend — wants to break up Girlz Only because of it. I hate this!"

That last outburst brought both of Otto's paws over his nose.

"I've gotta find some way to show them. I'm gonna show them all!"

Lily stopped for a breath. Otto peered out cautiously from underneath one paw.

"Oh — and I'm gonna show them it's a God thing too. Of course."

It might have been her imagination, she decided later, but at that moment it sure looked like Otto was rolling his eyes.

Lily propped herself up against her stuffed panda, China, to think. No ideas came — just flashes of scenes from the whole day. There was Shad bobbing his bandana-clad head to the music in the cafeteria and Kresha grinning from earlobe to earlobe. She remembered Ashley looking shocked when she found out the project really was Lily's idea and suggesting an in-school Christmas party.

Lily thought about how she had told Ashley that she and her officers could pull off just about anything.

"That's it!" she said out loud.

Lily bolted up on the bed so suddenly that Otto yipped. Standing up on the mattress, Lily jumped, laughing with every landing.

"That's it! We'll throw a major party and then nobody is gonna laugh at me — or try to change me — or blame stuff on me — "

There was a knock on the door. She was in mid-bounce when it opened.

"O-kay," Art said. "Whatever." He produced the phone. "Some guy for you."

"Ian!" Lily said.

She snatched the receiver out of his hand. Art left the room muttering, "The adolescent thing must be a whole other gig with girls."

"Hey," Ian said to Lily. "You wanna meet at the public library tomorrow — work on our geography thingies?"

"Yes!" Lily said. "And have I got a major idea to tell you!"

Lily made sure the table was set, the dishwasher was emptied, and Dad's newspaper was next to his chair when her parents got home.

That would make it a lot easier to talk them into letting her go to the library the next day.

"Reni going with you?" Mom said at the dinner table.

"No," Lily said. "Could somebody pass the celery sticks?" She didn't want to think about Reni right now — not when she was feeling so on top of things again.

"Is that *guy* goin' with ya?" Joe said in a high-pitched voice.

"Oh, you mean Ian?" Art said.

"Who's Ian?" Dad said, blinking vaguely and patting his pocket for his glasses — which, of course, weren't there.

"That's her boyfriend," Joe said.

"He is *not*!" Lily said.

"Don't have a coronary," Art said.

"Leave her alone, guys," Mom said.

"Is somebody going to tell me who this boy is?" Dad said.

"No," Joe said. "Interrogate her, Dad."

"He's my vice president," Lily said.

That got Mom and Dad trading looks across the table. But it was okay. *I'm gonna show them*, Lily thought. *I'm gonna show them all.*

The next day, Ian was already at the library when Lily arrived. That was a good thing, since Mom came in with her to make sure he'd shown up and that Lily wasn't going to be alone. Her face was already blotchy from that. When Mom said into her ear, "He *is* pretty cute, Lil," she went all the way red. She could feel it.

"Just kidding," Mom whispered as she turned around to leave. "You sure don't need a boyfriend — on top of everything else you've got going on."

When she was gone — finally — Lily hurried over to Ian.

"Does your family drive you nuts sometimes?" she said.

"Yeah. This morning my little brother wakes me up sliding a pencil up my nose!"

"Gross!"

He grinned and she grinned, and Lily realized how easy it was to talk to him. It wasn't even like talking to a boy.

"Are you gonna tell me your idea?" he said.

Quickly, being careful not to arouse a shush from the librarians at the counter, Lily filled him in on her conversation with Ashley and her decision to go after the Christmas party project.

"Wow," he said when she was finished. "That's huge."

"You don't think we can do it?"

His face slowly melted into a grin. "Of course we can do it," he said. "We're awesome."

He pushed his geography notebook aside and opened another binder, one that had Class Officer Business written on the front of it.

"Too bad Suzy's not here," Ian said. "She could take notes."

The mention of one of her Girlz gave Lily a pang. She shoved it aside like it was one of Ian's notebooks. At least she'd see Suzy when they did officer stuff, even if Girlz Only did dissolve—

"Hey," Ian whispered, "isn't that the girl you hang out with? What's her name—Reni?"

Lily whirled around to see where Ian was pointing. Reni had just walked in. Lily waved to her and motioned for her to come over.

But Reni's eyes flashed from Lily to Ian and back to Lily, where they clearly said, *Forget it, traitor. If you want to talk, you come to me.*

Then Reni gave her head a deliberate toss, beads clacking against each other as her numerous braids flew.

"Did she just blow you off?" Ian whispered.

"Yeah. She's jealous of me being all involved in officer stuff."

"Ah," Ian said, nodding like a wise old man. "She's probably too sensitive. Girls are like that—I mean, you know, most girls. Not you."

They turned back to the blank page of the notebook in front of them, but no sooner had Ian written *Christmas Party Project* at the top than there was a bunch of noise in the vicinity of the front door.

"Is there anybody we know who *isn't* gonna come in here today?" Ian said.

It was the ABCs — Ashley, Bernadette, Benjamin, and Chelsea — in outfits that would have sent Deputy Dog scurrying for her stack of referrals. The waistband of Benjamin's jeans was halfway down his fanny, plaid boxer shorts on partial display. The three girls had on almost identical tight, hip-hugging jeans and tops that looked as if they'd been painted on them.

"We could pretend we don't see them," Ian said.

"Yeah," Lily said. But then she shook her head. "No," she said, "we're the leaders. We should be better than they are."

"Yeah." Ian grinned. "'Cause we *are* better than they are."

When the ABCs finally got semi-settled at a table by the magazine rack, Lily and Ian went over to them, Ian with his hands parked casually in his pockets, Lily snapping a scrunchie around her hair so they wouldn't be tempted to inject their usual bad-hair-day comments.

"Hey, guys," Ian said. "You working on your projects too?"

The ABCs looked at each other and laughed for no apparent reason.

"We don't have to work on our projects," Bernadette said. "They're all done."

"Already?" Lily said.

More laughter. Lily felt like somebody had just told a joke she didn't get.

"We're quick," Benjamin said. "Just a coupla flicks of the wrist — "

Ashley smacked him on the arm, and Bernadette told him, "Shut up!" Chelsea tried to clap her hand over his mouth, but he dodged her.

"So — " Ian said. "What *are* you doing here?"

"We just wanted an excuse to get out of the house," Ashley said.

Ian grinned. "Yeah, I hear you," he said. "Me and Lily were just talking about that." He nudged Lily with his elbow.

"Oh — yeah," Lily said. "My little brother was driving me nuts."

Ian gave her an approving smile. Lily felt like she'd told a lie.

Still, the ABCs were no longer looking at them quite so much like they wished they'd disappear into the atmosphere.

"Okay," Ian said, "I gotta know — how'd you get your projects done so fast? Me and Lily have barely started."

Ashley and Chelsea giggled. Bernadette and Benjamin looked at each other. He raised his eyebrows at her. She shook her head. Lily wasn't sure, but she thought she'd witnessed an entire conversation.

"We're good," Benjamin said — and the laughter erupted again.

"Well, we're not," Ian said. "We better get back to work. Check you guys later."

"Hey, wait," Ashley said. "What about the Christmas party?" She narrowed her very blue eyes, thick with makeup, at Lily.

"We're working on it," Lily said.

"Even as we speak," Ian said. That sobered the ABCs up.

"You're actually going to try to get us a party?" Benjamin said.

"Why not?" Ian said.

"Sweet," Benjamin said. He put his palm up for Ian to slap with his.

"Wow," Lily whispered to Ian when they were back at their table. "He acted like he liked you."

"Yeah. My dad says that's what politics is about."

"Politics?"

"Yeah," Ian said. "We're elected officials. That makes us politicians. It's our job to make people like us so they'll trust us."

"Ashley Adamson is never gonna like me," Lily said. "And I sure don't trust her."

"Me neither," Ian said. "Did you know she cheats on tests? I've seen her."

Lily stared at Ian for a minute, visions of Ashley dropping her test paper on the floor for Ben to pick up — of asking Lily to change her answer — flashing fast in her head like a music video scene. "Yeah — " she said. "I think I have too."

"They probably all do — all four of them. They probably just copied some people's projects from last year and are gonna turn them in. How's Ms. Ferringer gonna know? This is her first year of teaching."

"That's awful!"

Ian nodded and picked up his pen.

"Shouldn't we be doing something about people cheating?" she said. "We're the class leaders. Aren't we supposed to, like, lead?"

Ian's eyes got patient like Dad's did when he was explaining fractions to Joe.

"Politicians don't tell on people," he said. "Not unless they're enemies. Then they *try* to find bad stuff to tell about them."

"They *are* the enemy," Lily said.

"No — we hafta keep them on our side if this Christmas party's gonna work."

He nodded at the still-empty sheet of paper with the party heading. But Lily felt like something was pulling her in another direction.

"But I thought we were supposed to make a difference," she said.

Ian gave the paper a tap with his pen. "This is gonna make a huge difference. I bet no other officers have ever even tried to get this for their class."

"Oh, yeah, huh?" Lily said.

She closed her eyes. She could see herself standing on the stage in the gym, looking proudly down at the seventh-grade class as they applauded her — and Ian and Suzy and Zooey and Lee — for throwing a party they'd never forget. And in the back of the gym would be Mom and Dad all misty-eyed, nodding so she'd know they recognized her gift as a leader. Oh — and just below the stage would be Reni, begging her to take her back as best friend —

"Okay," Lily said out loud, and the librarian said, "Shush!"

Ian grinned and pulled the cap off of his pen.

Chapter 8

It was hard seeing Reni at church the next day, especially since Reni refused to see Lily. Suzy, who always came to church with Reni, darted her dark eyes back and forth as if she were being pulled in two directions like a tug-of-war rope. Lily felt sorry for her. She stopped looking at Suzy so she wouldn't feel like Lily wanted her to come over to her side.

There aren't going to be any sides once they see that I'm right, Lily told herself.

On Monday morning, Lily went straight to Ms. Ferringer and asked if they could hold an urgent officers' meeting during lunch. Ms. Ferringer got the usual amused look on her face, but it didn't bother Lily now. Ms. Ferringer was going to be the first one to admit she was wrong about how important this was.

By then it was too late to check at the bench to see if any of the Girlz were there. As the warning bell rang, Lily was kind of glad. If they weren't, it'd be way too painful.

All morning, Reni avoided Lily, and Lily caught Suzy looking at her from time to time, eyes drooping like a puppy's. But when Lily looked back, Suzy always glanced anxiously at Reni and then buried her head in a book. By lunchtime, an empty spot had opened up in Lily. How, she wondered, could a space with nothing in it hurt so much?

At lunchtime, without Reni around, Suzy looked a little less like she was about to be hit by a car. Zooey, of course, ran *at* the car head-on.

"Lily, I hate it that there aren't any Girlz anymore!" she said. "Every time I think about it, I start crying."

"Come on, Zo," Lily said, "we haven't broken up."

"Reni says we have."

That made the empty spot bigger, but Lily shook her head. "Reni doesn't know everything. You'll see—she's gonna change her mind."

Zooey looked at Suzy, who looked down into her lap.

"What?" Lily said.

Zooey looked at Suzy again, but Suzy was staring intently at the tip of her pencil.

"Reni says she's never coming to Girlz again," Zooey said. "And she says she doesn't give the rest of us two weeks before we all drop out too."

Lily felt herself sag. "Reni said that?"

Zooey nodded. "She also said—"

"Never mind," Lily said. "I don't want to hear any more."

To herself she added, *Reni's going to see. She has to.* Then she cleared her throat and said, "The meeting will now come to order."

Taking turns with the parts they'd divided between them, Lily and Ian revealed their plan to the group. There would be a seventh-grade Christmas party during sixth period on the last day before Christmas vacation, complete with music, games, prizes for the most holiday spirit shown, and food; everything would be all planned out so nothing could go wrong.

When they were finished, Lily and Ian grinned at each other, and Lily felt better than she had all day. Lee, Suzy, and Zooey all nodded and said it was cool. Only Ms. Ferringer looked doubtful.

Ian leaned toward her. "Problem, Ms. Ferringer?" he said.

"I don't know," she said. "I mean, it sounds really good. But what about kids like Daniel and Leo who like to sabotage everything?"

"What's 'sabotage'?" Zooey said.

"It means mess it up," Ian told her. "But we'd have Deputy Dog — I mean, Officer Horn."

"Deputy who?" Ms. Ferringer said.

"What if we didn't let kids like Daniel and Leo come?" Lily said.

"They'd say we were discriminating," Ms. Ferringer said.

"Then we'd make it so they excluded themselves," Lily said. "Only people with all passing grades can come — and people with no U's in conduct." U's were for unsatisfactory behavior.

Ms. Ferringer twirled a finger in her hair. Ian nudged Lily. When she looked at him, his face was twisted into a question mark.

"What?" she whispered.

He picked up his pen and wrote furiously. *What are you doing? We didn't talk about this.*

Lily didn't have a chance to answer. Ms. Ferringer stopped twirling her curls and said, "Okay. If you put that provision in there, I'll go along with it."

"I don't know," Ian said. "That makes it more like school and less of a party. I don't just invite honor students to *my* parties."

Lee nodded in agreement. Zooey, however, blinked at him. "But it isn't *your* party, Ian," she said. "So that makes it different."

Wow, Lily thought. *Go, Zooey!*

"Some kids aren't gonna like that," Ian said. "They'll think we're being snobs."

"I think you're just being careful," Ms. Ferringer said. "I'm not comfortable with being responsible if trouble breaks out. Besides — " She gave one final twist to a corkscrew tendril above her ear. "I don't think Mr. Tanini is going to approve it any other way."

"Can't we at least try?" Ian said.

Lily found herself staring at him. He was sounding like Joe when he was begging to be allowed to stay up another hour.

"Why don't we vote on it?" she said.

Everybody voted "Aye" except Ian. For a few minutes, he wouldn't look at anybody.

"Can we present it tomorrow?" Lily said. "Can you have it typed up by then, Suzy?"

"You can use my computer," Ms. Ferringer said.

"Let's say we all meet here at the beginning of lunch and take it to him in the cafeteria like we did last time," Lily said. "We probably should all try to dress businesslike."

"Do I have to wear a tie?" Lee said.

Lily was so startled to hear him say something that she didn't notice at first that Ian was coming back into the discussion.

"You know what?" he said. "I have a computer at home — why don't I just type the proposal up tonight? Then Suzy doesn't have to wait in line for Ms. Ferringer's computer."

"There's not much of a line," Ms. Ferringer said with one of her throaty chuckles. "Except for you guys, I'm the only one who uses it."

"But what about — " Lily started to say.

Ian put his hand on her arm. "That's okay. I'll just do it at home."

Lily wanted to say, *What about Ashley and Benjamin?* but Ian filled up the rest of the meeting time getting the notes from Suzy.

Besides, what she saw after lunch period chased that from her mind.

She hurried to her locker when the bell rang to get her math book. There at *her* locker, right below Lily's, was Reni — with Monique. That wouldn't have been so bad except that when Reni saw Lily, she simply said — in a chilly voice — "Hello, Lily," and then nudged Monique as if they had some secret joke. They scurried off together like two best friends. The empty spot inside of Lily widened like a gulf.

She filled it with preparations for the next day's presentation. She spent thirty minutes that night picking out an outfit—a jumper and her most understated top. High heels would have made the ensemble perfect, but since asking Mom to buy her a pair of shoes was out of the question, she pulled the next best thing out of her closet, a pair of leather boots with thick heels she could at least pretend were pumps.

She was considering asking Dad if she could borrow a spare pair of his glasses when the phone rang. She dove for it before Joe or Art could get to it, just in case it was Ian. It was.

"You ready for tomorrow?" he asked. She could hear his excitement.

"Yeah," she said. "You want to meet in the morning and go over our parts?"

"You know, I was thinking," he said. "Why don't I get there early and give it to Mr. Tanini before school so he can read it before lunch. Then when we meet with him, he can tell us his decision then."

"I love it!" Lily said. "You want me to meet you at the office like at 7:30?"

"That's okay," Ian said. "Sleep in. I'll just drop it off."

"Oh," Lily said. "That's okay, too, I guess."

She felt a foggy disappointment as they hung up.

"Trouble with your man?" Art said, slipping an arm past her to take the phone.

"He's *not* my man!" Lily said.

Art stopped and looked at her closely. "You really like this guy, don't you?"

"He's *not* my boyfriend!" Lily said. She was on the verge of stomping her foot.

"I just said you like him—you know, like a friend."

"Oh," Lily said. "Well, yeah—I mean, can't I have a boy for a friend?"

"Sure. A lot of my friends are girls I won't ever date." Art deftly tossed the phone from one hand to the other. "Poor things. I know they all want me as a steady, but I can't please everyone."

"Barf," Lily said. She pretended to stick her finger down her throat and started back toward her room.

"Hey, Lil-Meister," Art said.

"Huh?" Lily said.

"Guy friends are totally different from girl friends except in one respect — they ain't perfect, any more than girls are. If this cat messes up somehow, just remember, we guys are only human too."

"*Huh?*" Lily said.

But Art was already walking away, punching in the number of the latest girlfriend who "wanted him."

Back in her room, Lily thought about that while she got out her talking-to-God journal. Ian *had* seemed pretty close to the perfect friend up 'til now. Even now, he hadn't really messed up. She just had a funny feeling about him.

"It's just 'cause of Reni," she told Otto. "Now it's hard to trust anybody."

Otto just eyed the pen she was uncapping.

"I have to act like the leader," she went on. "I can't be all petty. When Reni sees that I really *am* a good leader and I'm gonna stick with my gift, I'll forgive her." She snapped her fingers. "Just like that."

That felt better. It had to be because God approved.

The next day was like the one before, with Reni snubbing her and showing up with Monique at every turn and Zooey and Suzy and Kresha running back and forth between them like balls in a pinball machine. Only today, Lily stayed calm and refused to let the empty space get any bigger. She concentrated on the party project.

During third period, she slipped Ian a note on her way to the pencil sharpener. Mrs. Reinhold didn't catch her because she was busy having a discussion up at the front with Chelsea and Ashley.

Did you get the proposal to Mr. Tanini? it said.

Ian grinned at her and nodded, and on her way back from the pencil sharpener, he slipped her a note.

Do chickens have beaks? his said. *Of course I did. See you at lunch.*

It seemed like lunch would never come. When it did, Lily put Zooey's hair in a bun for her and buttoned Suzy's top button so she'd look more like somebody on *West Wing* and led the way to the cafeteria. This time when they passed through, a couple of people clapped. At their table, the ABCs pounded silently on the tabletop and whisper-chanted "Par-ty. Par-ty. Par-ty."

"See," Ian said into her ear. "We're politicians. Our public loves us."

Mr. Tanini gave them a broad smile when he saw them, and Lily was sure his bald head was shining more brightly than usual. He shook each of their hands, which took an eternity. It was all Lily could do not to say, "Well? Can we do it?"

Finally he got around to saying, "First let me tell you that I was very impressed, once again, with the professionalism of your proposal."

"Oh!" Zooey said. "So does that mean we get to have the party?"

Ian gave Lily a sour look. Lily had to admit, Zooey had a lot to learn about being a politician. That probably wasn't her God gift.

"Not quite," Mr. Tanini said. "While I think your plan is very well thought out, I see a huge margin for trouble that frankly I'm hesitant to risk."

"What's he talking about?" Zooey whispered to Lily.

"Kids are going to be so jazzed about it, nobody's going to make trouble," Ian said. "What we're trying to do is get kids to see that the administration trusts them."

"I'm not sure some of our kids *can* be trusted," Mr. Tanini said. "No matter what the circumstances."

"But those kinds of kids probably won't be there anyway," Lily said.

"How do you figure that?" Mr. Tanini said.

"The part about only people with passing grades and no conduct U's getting to come," Lily said.

Mr. Tanini looked at her blankly. "Did I miss that part?"

"It was right in there," Lily said.

"Tell me about it," Mr. Tanini said.

Lily looked at Ian. He didn't give her the usual go-ahead nod. He was watching his foot swing back and forth in front of him.

"Anybody?" Mr. Tanini said.

"Um — me, I guess," Lily said. "We had it in there that you could go to the party only if you had all passing grades and no conduct U's. Teachers would turn in a list of who didn't meet the requirements two days before, and then those kids would go to study hall while the rest of us went to the party."

"Excellent idea," Mr. Tanini said. "Like an incentive."

"What's an incentive?" Zooey mumbled. Lily decided she was really going to have to work with her on her vocabulary — maybe at the next Girlz Only meeting. That is, if they ever had another one.

"Interesting," Mr. Tanini said. "I'm surprised I didn't see that in your proposal — I'd have given my immediate approval."

"It's in there," Lily said.

Ian coughed. "Um — it might not be," he said. "I might have left it out — accidentally."

"It's an essential part of the project," Mr. Tanini said. "You put that in writing, and I'll let you have your party. And put in there that the requirements are to be posted in every classroom on colored fliers so nobody can miss them. We don't want people hollering that they didn't know." His eyes twinkled. "This is wonderful. There's still time for people to bring their grades up and clean up their acts. We have, what, two weeks until party time?"

"Yes, sir!" Zooey said, beaming.

Lee and even Suzy were nodding like they had springs for necks.

Lily, however, was watching Ian. He was standing there with his hands in his pockets, looking everywhere but at her. She plucked at

71

his sleeve and pulled him away from where Zooey was babbling away to Mr. Tanini.

"You left it out on purpose, didn't you?" she said to him.

He started to shake his head, but when he finally looked at her, he said, "I had to try it."

"But we almost didn't get to do the party because of that!"

Ian grinned. "We still get to do it. And what if he *had* said okay without the grade thing? We might have gotten to do it without ticking anybody off."

"But that's *not* what we voted on!"

Ian sighed like she was really trying his patience. "It's called strategy, Lily," he said. "You can't always give in — you have to take some risks."

"It could have messed the whole thing up — " Lily stopped herself, and she started over. "I know you aren't perfect, and I don't expect you to be."

"Huh?"

"But you *could* have really messed that up."

"Not a chance," Ian said. "I knew you'd bring up the grade thing if he started to turn us down. Then I could say I left it out by accident." Ian shrugged. "It worked."

"But — that doesn't seem very right," Lily said.

"Hey, Robbins."

Lily tossed her head impatiently toward the voice. It was Ashley, clustered at her table with the rest of her gang.

"I'm kind of busy right now," Lily said.

"Whatcha need, Ash?" Ian said.

"So — what about our party?" 'Ash' said. Her upper lip was in full curl. Ms. Ferringer could have twirled it around her finger. "Do we get to have the party?"

"Oh, yeah, baby," Ian said.

And then he gave Lily his biggest grin yet.

Chapter 9

By Friday, Lily could say that Ian had been wrong about one thing: not many people seemed too upset about the requirements for attending the party. Kids who had never even looked at Lily before were coming up to her in the halls, saying things like:

"Way to go, Robbins."

"You guys totally rock."

And her favorite — "I thought the officer thing was, like, a big joke. You guys are actually getting stuff for us!"

At one point, before school on Friday, there were so many people crowded at what used to be the Girlz bench that it had suddenly become the officers' meeting place. Kresha had to tug on Lily's sleeve several times before Lily turned and saw her.

"Is anything wrong?" Lily said.

Kresha looked so frantic her eyes couldn't be still, and she was wringing her hands like a washcloth.

"What is it?" Lily said.

"No music!" Kresha said.

"What do you mean no music? What are you talking abo—" Lily grabbed Kresha by both shoulders. "There's no music for lunch?"

Kresha shook her head.

"Why *not*?"

"Reni — she tell me she do it. Then now she tell me she *not* do it — on purple — to show you — I don't know — "

All of Kresha's progress in English vanished, but Lily understood enough to set her heart into a pounding panic.

"She told you she'd pick the music and then she didn't, on purpose, just so she could show me I'm not a leader? Is that what you're saying?"

Kresha nodded. "I tell her today I try to pick songs. But she say she take all CDs to her house — "

"Oh, no!" Lily said.

The windup in her voice started Kresha crying. Lily grabbed her own hair with both hands. "Please don't cry, Kresha," she said. "I'm already freaked out."

"I mess up everything for you!"

"It's not your fault," Lily said. "I'll fix it." She stopped and let go of her hair. Of course she would fix it. She was the leader. She'd figure something out. And that was going to show Reni better than anything.

"Go blow your nose," Lily said. "You've got snot all over."

Kresha nodded even as she smeared her nose on her sleeve. Lily grabbed Suzy with one hand and Ian with the other.

"Go to the restroom with Kresha," she said to Suzy. "Ian, I gotta talk to you."

"What's up?" Ian said. He looked a little annoyed. "I was right in the middle of something."

"We have a situation," Lily said.

As she filled him in, the annoyed look disappeared, replaced by the same look Lily knew she had on hers — almost panic.

"We have to fix it," she said.

"Okay — let me think." Ian put his hand up to his forehead, then snapped his fingers.

"Lee!" he said. "He always has CDs in his backpack. He listens to some pretty weird stuff, but there's probably something in there we can use."

"Get him!" Lily said.

Ian was already on his way. Lily prayed like there was no tomorrow.

When Ian came back, he had Lee with him, and he was grinning.

"He's gonna pick out some songs for us by fourth period," Ian said. "And he's gonna help Kresha at lunch. It's all taken care of."

"You rock, Lee," Lily said. "You saved our lives!"

Lee just nodded modestly.

Reni had just tried to humiliate Lily in front of everybody. It was going to be harder than she thought to forgive her, once she finally saw it Lily's way. And she would—Lily was sure of that.

She felt like she was sitting on a pincushion until fourth period, when Lee handed her a stack of CDs. While Ms. Ferringer shouted out the roll and looked for her pen, Lily looked through the stack.

Ian had been right. Lee listened to some weird stuff—at least things Lily had never heard of. It was sort of pointless to even pretend she was approving his choices, since she didn't know one from the other.

When Ms. Ferringer finally set them loose to work on their projects, Ian came over, took the seat Reni had vacated to go to the library, and said, "Did my boy come through?"

"Yep," Lily said. "Here's the stuff."

She handed him the stack. Ian glanced through it, grunting and nodding—until he came to one entitled *EMINEM*.

"Back the truck up!" he said. "We can't play this—every song on here's got cussing and other stuff in it. We would be *so* busted."

"Give it back to him!" Lily said.

"He went to the library."

"Let me have it, then," Lily said. "I'll throw it in my locker."

When she took it from him, she saw that her hand was shaking.

Right after fourth period, Ian and Lily ran down to the office with the CDs. Kresha was already there, white-faced as she put on her headphones. Only the sight of Lily and a laid-back Lee got her to take a deep breath and start the first CD.

"We agreed to have two kids here for this," one of the secretaries said to them. "I see four of you."

"We're going, ma'am," Ian said, nudging Lily toward the door.

"Wow," she heard the secretary say. "Finally, a kid with some decent manners."

"You make everybody like you," Lily said.

"I told you," Ian said. "I'm a politician."

But he was a nervous politician. Lily could see that as they tried to eat their lunches. With each new song that came on, they looked around to make sure somebody liked it. Some of the more off-the-wall kids — like Daniel and Leo and Marcie McCleary — were digging it today. Ashley and Chelsea and Bernadette kept wrinkling their noses — but at least there was *something* coming out of those speakers. The officers had come so close to blowing it, Lily didn't even want to think about it. And what was worse — it was Reni who had tried to make them blow it.

Although the empty spot stayed in Lily, the next week and a half was such a flurry of activity getting ready for the party, she didn't have much time to think about it. There were the requirement fliers to put up in the classrooms. Food had to be ordered from the cafeteria — which did make some pretty good chocolate-chip cookies and fairly edible cupcakes. Decorations needed to be designed for the art classes to make. There were games to plan and music to pick out.

A lot of different people from the seventh grade volunteered to help, but no one put in more time than the officers themselves and Kresha. Reni, on the other hand, did nothing. She seemed way too involved with Monique to bother with anything else.

I don't think she even spent that much time with me when we were friends, she wrote to God one night. Then she changed the subject in her head. Every time she thought about Reni and Girlz Only, the empty space inside her only got bigger.

But it was hard to avoid the subject. Even Mom brought it up one night when Lily went down to the family room to kiss her and Dad good night. Mom was wrapping presents to send to out-of-town relatives, and she had to take the tape dispenser out of her mouth to kiss Lily back. With the room addition and the adoption all in the works, this was the first sign of Christmas Lily had seen around the house.

"How's everything going?" Mom said. "I haven't heard you talk about the Girlz in a while."

"Oh, they're fine," Lily said. "Everybody's busy with—different stuff."

"You still meeting every day after school?"

"Um, not so much," Lily said. "G'night."

"Whose idea was that?" Mom said.

"It just kind of happened," Lily said.

Mom put her scissors down. Dad looked up from the book he was reading and nibbled at the earpiece on his glasses.

"Are you okay with that?" Mom said.

"We'll get back together," Lily said. She was feeling so empty, her voice even sounded hollow.

"That's not what I asked you. Are *you* okay with it?"

"I miss them, I guess," Lily said. "But I'm busy too."

"Was there trouble?" Mom said.

"It's okay," Lily said. "You said you thought I was involved in too much stuff anyway. Maybe this is God saying I need to concentrate on being class president."

"We didn't mean for you to give up your friends, Lilliputian," Dad said.

"I didn't give them up! Suzy and Kresha and Zooey and I are still close!"

"And Reni?" Dad said.

Why was it, Lily wondered, that he could be so absentminded until there was something she *wanted* him to miss and then he was so alert she couldn't get anything past him?

"I think she has a new best friend," Lily said, tears in her voice.

"Oh, Lil," Mom said. "I'm so sorry."

"She'll come back," Lily said. "I know she will."

But when she got back to her room, Lily cried until she fell asleep.

The next day brought them closer to the deadline for teachers to turn in their lists. In fifth-period math, Mr. Chester was taking the incentive thing pretty seriously. He gave a pop quiz.

Luckily, Lily was ready. She was studying more than ever these days just to be on the safe side with Mom and Dad *and* because of the party. Besides, that was what leaders did. They set an example.

Marcie McCleary obviously didn't follow it. Unlike Ms. Ferringer, Mr. Chester was like a watchdog during tests and quizzes, and he caught her gawking at Lee's paper. Her paper was torn up — and the large F and U written in his grade book. The rest of the class whispered among themselves as Mr. Chester collected the papers.

"Hey," Benjamin said above the hissing. "That means she doesn't get to go to the party."

"Too bad, McCleary," Chelsea said with a smirk.

But Ashley turned to Marcie and looked almost sympathetic. "It's a stupid rule anyway," she said. "You just gotta be more careful if you're gonna cheat."

"No," Mr. Chester said, "she just needs to study so she doesn't *have* to cheat."

Lily looked at Ian. He nodded toward Ashley and gave Lily an I-told-you-so look.

By the end of the day, word had gotten around that teachers were deliberately trying to make sure kids had their stuff together.

"It's like the party is some reward for being good little children or something," Benjamin said to Lily at the lockers after school.

"So," Lily said. "Be a good little child and you don't have to worry."

"I *don't* have anything to worry about," Benjamin said, and walked off still wiggling his eyebrows.

"Yikes, Lily," Zooey said. "You really stood up to him."

I did, didn't I? Lily thought. But to Zooey she said, "That's what leaders do."

"Stood up to Reni, then," Kresha said. She bobbed her head toward the end of the row of lockers.

Reni was there with Monique. She had obviously seen the Girlz, because she seemed to be stalling until they were gone before she went to her locker.

"You oughta talk to her, Lily," Zooey said. "I think she's just being stubborn."

"No," Lily said. "She won't listen to me anyway." She didn't tell them that by this time Friday, Reni was going to be begging her to be best friends with her again.

Everything was under control with the party. The only thing Lily didn't have a handle on was her project for geography. She'd intended to spend a lot of time on it, but every time she and Ian got together to work on theirs, they ended up talking about officer business. The projects were due the next day, and she still had a lot of work to do.

She said a silent prayer of thanks when Mom and Dad announced at supper that they were going to a seminar on adopting older kids and wouldn't be in until late. That meant she could cram to get her project done without having to do it under her covers with a flashlight.

But there was more left to do than she'd thought. She was still finishing up the last section — "The Future of France" — when she heard the garage door open. There was no point diving under the blankets and pretending to be asleep now. They'd probably already seen the light in her window anyway. Besides, she had only a few more paragraphs to go — and the table of contents — and the bibliography.

She yawned and shook her aching hand and kept working. As she predicted to Otto, there was a tap on her door about thirty seconds later.

"What are you still doing up?" Mom said. "It's almost eleven o'clock."

"I'm practically done," Lily said. "Just give me twenty more minutes, okay?"

"What are you working on?" Dad said over Mom's shoulder.

"My geography report. Want to see what I've done so far?"

Mom picked up the almost-finished report, but she gave it only a passing glance. "You've had this assignment for a while, Lil," she said. "Why did you procrastinate?"

"What about all those trips to the library?" Dad said.

Lily felt like somebody being questioned on *Law and Order*. She scrunched up her shoulders. "I didn't leave it *all* until the last minute — "

"I think I know the problem," Mom said.

"You finish that up and get your party over with," Dad said. "Then this weekend, we have a date to sit down and look at your priorities."

Lily wasn't sure what priorities were, but at the moment they didn't sound like something that was going to go on her Christmas wish list.

"I'm using my gifts," Lily said. "I'm talking to God — "

"Like Dad said, we'll talk this weekend." Mom looked at Otto, who was dozing at Lily's feet. "And don't stay up too much longer. You're wearing Otto out."

Otto growled sleepily.

"At least *you're* still on my side," Lily said to him when they'd gone. It sure didn't seem like too many other people were.

Chapter
10

Lily had a hard time hauling herself out of bed the next morning, but she tried to look wide awake so Mom and Dad wouldn't have any more evidence that she wasn't handling all her responsibilities. But once she got to school, she dropped the act. She was bleary-eyed when she turned in her geography project during fourth period.

But being foggy-minded didn't keep her from feeling a pang when Reni's notebook passed through her hands on its way up the row. Even two weeks ago, Lily would have known everything Reni did about the Galapagos Islands, because they would have been working on their projects like they were connected with Velcro.

In the next row, Ms. Ferringer was at Ashley's desk looking through her project. "This is fabulous!" she was saying. "It's the best work you've done all year!"

"Look at Chelsea's," Marcie McCleary said. "Hers is, like, professional."

"Huh," Lily heard Reni mumble behind her. "Since when were they so creative?"

Lily automatically turned around and said, "Yeah, really. What's up with that?"

For a fraction of a second their two gazes met in agreement. But with a jerk, Reni brought the sheet music on her desk up in front of her face and walled off Lily.

By then, Ms. Ferringer was squealing over Ben's project. Her pitch went up a whole octave when she picked up Bernadette's. Within seconds, there was a note from Ian on Lily's desk.

They had them done in two days and they're totally good? he'd written. *I don't get it.*

Me neither, Lily wrote. *Something's weird.*

Lily got up as if to throw something in the trash and dropped the note on Ian's desk as she passed. She also had to walk by the ABCs — so she couldn't mistake the fact that all four of them were obviously holding back laughter. As she squeezed by them to get to her seat, she heard Ben mutter to Bernadette, "It's all about the inter — "

He stopped, though, and looked up at Lily. "What?" he said.

"Nothing!" she said, and moved on to her desk.

On her way, Lee tugged on her sleeve. "EMINEM," he said.

"What?"

"You dig EMINEM, man?" Benjamin said to Lee.

I love how you think everybody's talking to you, Benjamin, Lily thought.

Lee nodded at Ben and then homed in on Lily again. "My CD," he said.

"Oh," Lily said. "We couldn't use it — it's still in my locker."

"I need it," Lee said. And then he clamped his mouth shut as if he'd exhausted all his words for the day.

Lily finally got back to her desk. Moments later there was another note from Ian: *What did Ben say?*

I don't know, she wrote back. *'It's all about the inter' — whatever that is.*

I think I know, his next note read. *Can you come over to my house after school?*

Sure, Lily wrote.

This time as she delivered her reply, she caught Reni watching her. Her black eyes flashed in a way that made Reni look almost evil.

What's happening? Lily thought. *I so don't get it.*

And it *so* made her sad.

At least that afternoon after school, Lily had something to do besides sit at home and miss Girlz Only. It was pretty obvious by now that none of the Girlz had the heart to get together. Going to Ian's made the empty place inside seem a little smaller.

He lived in one of the newer neighborhoods in Burlington in a two-story brick house with perfectly squared-off hedges outside and everything shiny and new-smelling inside. Ian led Lily to the sparkly kitchen that was big enough to play hockey in, where they warmed up Hot Pockets in the microwave and then headed for the family room. Ian plopped himself down at a computer desk and rolled another chair over for Lily.

"So what are we doing?" Lily said as Ian began clicking keys and maneuvering the mouse.

"You remember you said Ben said something like, 'It's all about the inter' — ?"

"Yeah."

Just then, the computer announced to Ian that he had mail.

"You think he was gonna say 'Internet'?" Lily said.

"I don't think he meant interior decorating."

"But a lot of people got their information from the Net," Lily said. "That's where I got some of mine. Ms. Ferringer told us we could do that."

"Did you get a good look at their stuff?" Ian said as he continued to click and clack as images flashed by on the screen.

"No," Lily said.

"I did. I gotta admit that Marcie girl was right — they did look professional. Okay —" he pointed at the screen. "Here's Ethiopia —

that was Ashley's country." Ian leaned in and read silently, lips moving as he went.

What the heck's he doing? Lily thought. *I don't care about Ethiopia right now!*

"Whoa," Ian said. He sat back in the chair.

"What?" Lily said.

"This sounds exactly like what I read in her report. I mean — exactly."

Lily could feel her eyes going round. "You mean, like, she copied?"

"I'm thinking so. Let me check Ben's. He wrote about Turkey."

Lily was now as riveted to the screen as Ian was. She held her breath as he read.

"I can't say for sure," he told her, "but some of this stuff sounds familiar. Like I remember he wrote something about Constantinople being the 'glittering capital' — 'cause I thought, dude, he's like a poet or something."

"What about Chelsea's?" Lily said.

Ian went after it with the mouse again and came up with the same conclusion about Chelsea — and Bernadette.

"So that's why they got done so fast," Lily said.

"I told you I thought they were copying kids' papers from last year. This was even sneakier."

Lily swallowed hard. "So — what are we gonna do?"

"What do you mean, do?" Ian said as he exited from the Internet and reached for the rest of his Hot Pocket. Lily's was still on the plate, barely nibbled at.

"Don't we have to turn them in?" Lily said. "This is major cheating."

"But if we turn them in, they don't get to go to the party."

"So?" Lily said.

"So — they'll hate us for the rest of their natural lives."

Lily shrugged. "They already hate me."

"No, they don't," Ian said. "They've been pretty decent to you since we started all our officer stuff. You're totally getting to be popular. Haven't you picked up on that?"

"But it isn't fair to all of us that worked our tails off to just let them get away with it."

Ian chewed thoughtfully on the last bite of his Hot Pocket. Then he said, "So what if we turn them in, only we do it anonymously? That way they never know it was us."

"Is that honest?" Lily said.

"Courts use secret witnesses all the time!"

"How would we do it if we did it anonymously?"

Ian shrugged. "Easy. We type up a letter and put it in Ms. Ferringer's box."

"I don't know," Lily said.

"What is the big deal? It's Ms. Ferringer's job to nail them anyway — not ours."

"Is that the way politicians do it?"

"'Course it is."

Lily found herself twisting a curl around her finger the way Ms. Ferringer did. "I think we oughta pray about it first," she said.

"You can if you want," Ian said. "I don't pray."

"You don't?" Lily said. "How do you ever decide what you're supposed to do?"

"I don't know," Ian said. "I just know. I pay attention and figure out what's going on and then I just do whatever."

"Wow," Lily said.

"You want somethin' to drink?" Ian said.

Lily shook her head. When Ian had gone to the kitchen, she leaned back in the chair and closed her eyes. Something was way wrong with this picture. Way wrong.

She and Ian hung out for another thirty minutes, playing computer games. Lily got bored fast — that happened when you lost six games in a row. Besides, it was hard to concentrate with the whole cheating thing still bounding around in her mind. Ian, on the other hand, seemed to have forgotten about it.

When Mrs. Collins finally poked her head in and met Lily, she invited her to stay for the Chinese food she was going to order out. But Lily said no thanks and went for her boots.

"So — I'll have the note ready for Ms. Ferringer tomorrow morning," Ian said.

Lily shook her head. "You can go ahead and write it, but don't put it in her box 'til I get there, okay?"

"Oh, yeah, that's right. You gotta pray."

There was something about the edge in his voice that made Lily look up — just in time to see a lip quickly uncurl. In that instant, he looked an awful lot like Ashley.

When Lily waved good-bye to him from the sidewalk, she felt emptier than she'd felt yet. Something was getting weird, and she didn't know what to do about it. She couldn't even pray about it yet, because she couldn't get all the confusing pieces sorted out.

I want somebody to pray with, she thought as she stomped through a half-frozen clump of leaves. *The Girlz and I always prayed together.*

It was such a lonely thought that it made her shiver. Hunching her shoulders against the cold, Lily pushed it out of her mind.

The problem with *not* thinking about it was that she couldn't pray about it either. That night, as she tried to settle in with Otto, China, and her prayer journal, the only thoughts that would spill out onto the page were *Please, God, make Reni want to be friends with me again. Please, God, don't let the Girlz break up.* And *Please, God, take this empty place in my heart away.*

Since it hurt too much to pray those thoughts, she closed her book and absentmindedly gave Otto the pen to chew on. When Ian called to find out what she'd decided, she hadn't decided anything, and Otto had gotten green ink all over the sheets.

"So—if you don't know what to do and I *do*," Ian said, "why don't we just do it my way?"

"Okay," Lily said. "We'll turn in the note—only don't do it 'til I've read it this time, okay?"

Ian sounded a little offended when he hung up, but Lily was way too tired to care.

The next day, Lily met Ian at the very empty bench and read the note he'd typed.

> *Ben and Ashley and Chelsea and Bernadette probably copied their projects right off the Internet. You might want to check into that.*
> *Signed, Concerned Student*

Lily studied it for so long, Ian started sighing and shifting from foot to foot. Since she couldn't find anything really wrong with it, she finally gave him a nod. But it still didn't feel right.

"Would you quit stressing?" Ian said. "We're doing it this way so nobody has to pay except the people that *should* pay. Now—" He tucked the note into his pocket and looked around like they were about to hold up a convenience store. "When we get to the office, you put it in her box while I keep a lookout."

"For what?" Lily said.

"For one of them! We don't want them seeing us around there, or they'll put it together that it was us that told."

"You want me to go put on a disguise or something?" Lily said.

"Huh?"

"Nothing," Lily said. *Sarcasm*, she thought, *always works for Art, but it hardly ever works for me.*

Ian put his hands casually into his pockets and started a stroll toward the office. "Look nonchalant," he told Lily.

She tried, but she was anything but blasé about this. Her heart was pounding, and her palms had already gone clammy. It *felt* like they were going to hold up a store.

"It's all a game," Ian said close to her ear. "That's what politics is, mostly, my dad says — a game."

Lily stared at him for a second. He did look like he was having fun. She wasn't.

When they got to the office, Ian looked all around, though there was hardly anybody there yet. "Okay, go for it," he said. "If you don't come out in exactly one minute, I'll know something's wrong, and I'll come in. We oughta have some kind of signal in case you don't *want* me to come in — "

"Just give me the note," Lily said. "I'll be out in fifteen seconds."

"Don't attract any attention to yourself," Ian said. "Maybe you should of worn a hat — I mean, 'cause your hair kind of stands out."

Lily snatched the note out of his hand. *I don't care if we do get caught!* she thought. *You'd think we were the criminals!*

It took less than fifteen seconds to find Ms. Ferringer's box, push the note into it, and leave the office. But Ian was practically wringing his hands when she reached him.

"Did anybody see you?" he said.

"I don't think so."

"Nobody said anything? You didn't hear anybody breathing on the other side of the boxes or anything?"

"No!" Lily said. "You need to switch to decaf, Ian."

"You don't get it," Ian said. "We're gonna be like total outcasts if Ashley and them ever find out about this."

"I've gotta go to my locker," Lily said. "I'll see you third period."

She didn't give him a chance to suggest anything else. He was starting to grate on her. What she really wanted to do was be with her Girlz so she could vent about how Ian was freaking out —

But when she surveyed the bench from the bottom of the stairs, it was empty. The sad part was, she wasn't surprised.

Suzy, Zooey, and Kresha, when she saw them during the morning, were still friendly, but something had definitely changed. All three of them looked as if they were being pulled in opposite directions like Gumby dolls. Nobody seemed to have much to say, except Zooey, who chattered on about nothing in a high-pitched, nervous voice until Kresha threatened to stick a sock in her mouth. Reni, of course, wouldn't even look at Lily. By fourth period, Lily had seen her with Monique three times, laughing and whispering with her as if *they* were the ones who had been best friends since way back in elementary school.

When fourth period did come, Lily switched her attention to a more important issue. She watched as the ABCs trailed into geography class, almost late. They were showing no signs of having been punished yet. Ben was teasing Ashley by pulling on her sweater, and Chelsea and Bernadette were laughing and tugging him away. All was pretty much normal with them.

But Ms. Ferringer didn't look normal when she got there. There was mascara smudged under her eyes like she'd been crying, and she didn't even bother to open her grade book, much less start shouting out the roll when the bell rang. In fact, her face was so stony serious, the class quieted down on its own.

"Chelsea, Ashley, Benjamin, and Bernadette," she said. "I want to see all of you out in the hall, please."

"Why?" Ben said.

"Because I said so," Ms. Ferringer said.

One of the boys gave a low whistle, and somebody else muttered, "Kick tail, Ms. Ferringer." The ABCs didn't look too disturbed. Ashley even rolled her eyes at Ben as they followed Ms. Ferringer out, like this was a tremendous waste of her time.

When they were gone, Lily kept her eyes glued to the desktop. She wanted to look at Ian, but she knew he'd say that she had almost blown their cover or something.

Everybody else in the room broke into whispers. Out of the corner of her eye, Lily could see Ian joining them, hissing away as if he were as mystified as the rest of them. Lily didn't feel like pretending. The words *Please, God, let this turn out right* floated softly through her head.

"Hey, Lily, wake up," Marcie McCleary whispered. "They're coming back in."

Lily blinked her eyes open. None of the ABCs looked any different than they had when they'd left. Ms. Ferringer still appeared to be on the verge of bawling her eyes out. This time, Lily did look at Ian. His face was one big puzzle.

"All right," Ms. Ferringer said. "Read chapter six and answer the questions at the end of the chapter — and *no* talking. I am *not* in the mood."

Then she dropped into her chair, put her forehead in her hands, and stayed there the rest of the period.

There were few people in the room who didn't talk, or at least pass notes. Lily tried to read, but a story was piecing itself together all around her, and that was all that would fit into her mind.

"Somebody accused them of copying their projects off the Internet — "

"Whoever it was didn't have the guts to come forward — "

" — left her a note — "

"She can't do a thing to them — "

"She's not gonna search the whole stupid Internet trying to check up on them — "

" — gave them a warning — "

"Who *did* that? Who turned them in?"

About then, Lily had to cover her ears, or she knew she would have stood up and shouted, "I did it! I left the anonymous note — and I'm sorry I did — because now — they're getting *away* with it!"

Chapter

11

Lily bolted to her locker right after class so she wouldn't have to talk to anybody — but Ian was right on her heels.

"You know you almost gave us away, don't you?" he said in a voice so low she could barely hear him above the slamming of lockers all around them.

"I didn't say a word!"

"Shhhh!" Ian glanced over both shoulders and got closer to Lily. "It was so obvious you were freaking out. Why didn't you, like, join in the conversation?"

"Because I'm no good at lying," Lily said. She threw her geography book into the locker, smashing her brown-bag lunch. When she pulled it out, banana was already oozing out through the paper.

"People suspect you," Ian whispered. By now his eyes had narrowed to slits behind his glasses. He was looking more like Ashley all the time. "This one guy goes, 'What's up with Robbins? She's never that quiet.'"

"Thanks for sharing," Lily said through her teeth. She slammed her locker and tried to get around Ian, but he dodged and got right in her path.

"How come you're all mad?" he said.

"You aren't mad that they got away with it?" Lily said.

"Shut *up*!" he hissed. "You *want* to give us away?"

"Maybe I do," Lily said. "Let me get by — "

But Ian gave her a push, just hard enough to send her off balance so that she had to lean against the bank of lockers. She clung to her lunch and stared at him.

"You tell anybody, and I'll deny it," he said in his lowest voice yet. "I've worked too hard to get popular with everybody — and you're not gonna mess that up for me."

Then he turned around, shoved his hands into his pockets, and strolled away as if they'd had a nice little chat about what was on the hot lunch menu. Before he reached the stairwell, he said hi to ten people. One of them was Benjamin.

Somehow Lily got to the cafeteria without bursting into sobs. Once she got inside the door, it struck her that she had no one to eat with. Her eyes went automatically to the Girlz' old table, and there was Kresha, sitting alone. A glance around revealed that Suzy and Zooey were still in the lunch line. Lily ran to Kresha.

Kresha's face lit up so brightly, Lily almost *did* start to cry then. But she swatted away the tears and sank gratefully onto the bench across from her.

The light in Kresha's face darkened. "You are sad, Lily?"

Lily nodded.

"Why?"

"Because I'm so stupid!" Lily said.

"No — you are not stupit," Kresha said, spitting out the "t" that didn't belong there. "You are wery smart."

Lily shook her head miserably. "No — I *am* stupid," she said. "I thought I was this big leader, and I found out I'm not because I don't have any guts."

"What is 'guts'?" Kresha said.

"And I let being president mess up Girlz Only — and that messed up everything with Reni — and then I thought Ian was my friend but he only cares about Ian — and I thought he wanted to do big stuff for the class and make a difference, only all he cares about is — Ian." Lily took a breath and charged on. "And now there's this *other* mess that I can't even *tell* you about. Everything is so messed up, Kresha, and it's my fault — *again!* I try to pray and everything, and then it still turns out so *bad!*"

The way Kresha was watching her, lips echoing every few words that came out of her mouth, Lily was sure she hadn't understood more than half of it. But the empty space inside her was a little smaller, just because she'd gotten all of that out. She brushed away the few tears that had managed to escape and was about to add a few more sentences, when a shadow fell across the table. Lily looked up to see Ashley standing there. She didn't have to look to know that the rest of the ABCs were right behind her.

"Hey, Lil," Ashley said. "What's up?"

Lily stared.

"Only a couple days 'til the party," Bernadette said from over Ashley's shoulder. "Me and Chelsea and Ashley are all gonna dress alike — we got the cutest Santa hats."

"Don't tell her *everything*!" Chelsea said, playfully smacking at Bernadette.

Lily looked blankly at Kresha, who looked back with just as clueless a face.

"I gotta tell you something, Robbins," Benjamin said, propping his foot up on the bench Lily was sitting on. "I used to think you were a hopeless nerd nobody could change."

"Be-en!" Ashley said.

"Yeah — but it's okay because I don't think that anymore," Benjamin said. "You and Ian and Lee — you guys rock."

"Now, those other two," Bernadette said, rocking her hand back and forth as if Suzy and Zooey were questionable, "they *might* be hopeless."

"You gu-uys!" Ashley said. "I mean, ouch—those are her friends."

Bernadette leaned in so that her powdered little nose was inches from Lily's. "I'd dump them, Lily," she said. "They're probably really nice and everything, but they're never gonna be as popular as you are. They're just gonna hold you back."

She gave her curled hair a shake and straightened up again. It occurred to Lily that Bernadette had made that whole little speech as if Kresha hadn't even been there. Only by gritting her teeth did Lily keep herself from exploding.

"We gotta go," Ashley said. "You wanna eat lunch with us tomorrow?"

"I have an officers' meeting at lunch tomorrow," Lily said woodenly.

"Dude, you guys are, like, slave drivers," Ben said.

Then he nodded to his harem, and they dutifully followed after him. If Lily hadn't been able to eat her squashed banana before, she could barely think about it now without gagging.

Kresha was watching her. "They like you, Lily," she said.

"Gross me out and make me icky," Lily said. "Kresha—I *am* stupid."

For the rest of the afternoon, the thoughts chased each other in a circle in Lily's head. All she could think about was what those wretched people had gotten away with, the idea that they thought she was like them, and the fact that if she didn't give Ms. Ferringer the details about their cheating, she *was* like them.

And she was like Ian.

And she was no longer like her Girlz.

It was a good thing the thoughts started over again from there, or she would have cried all over her pre-algebra equations.

In sixth period, Lily was about midway through the thought circle for the fifteenth time when a Girlz Gram made its way to her desktop. It was the first one she'd gotten in weeks.

Hoping desperately that it was from Reni, Lily tore it open. It was in Kresha's slightly funky handwriting.

Meet — Zooey house — after school — today, it said.

Lily gave Kresha a puzzled look, but she just shrugged and smiled.

She must have told Zooey what I said at lunch, Lily thought. *At least the three of us can talk. Maybe I won't feel so bad then.*

As she tucked the note into her binder, Lily added, *Thank you, God.*

It at least gave Lily something to look forward to. She didn't see Kresha or Zooey once after school, but she skipped a little as she hurried toward Zooey's house alone. It didn't matter if Zooey's mother hadn't fixed cheese balls or even put chips in a bowl for them — as long as she could feel like at least some of them were the Girlz again.

Mrs. Hoffman hollered from the kitchen for Lily to come on in when she knocked. Lily just murmured thanks as she headed for the basement door. There was *another* person she'd messed up with. Would the list never end?

She was preparing her apology speech for Mrs. Hoffman as she went down the steps toward the wonderful musty smell of Zooey's basement, so she was surprised to look up and see Suzy in the pink beanbag, smiling shyly at her.

"You too?" Lily said.

Suzy nodded. "I was going nuts without this. I'm so glad Kresha thought of it."

Light shafted from the top of the stairs as the door opened.

"Your mom fixed us food on this short notice?" Lily said.

Zooey shook her head. Down the steps came Reni.

Lily felt herself sagging deeper into the beanbag. If Reni saw her, she was likely to turn and head right out of there.

But Reni didn't. She just stopped at the bottom of the steps and stared at Lily for a whole minute. Then she turned on Kresha as if she were going to snatch her nose off.

"You said *she* wasn't going to be here!" she said, pointing to Lily.

"I lie," Kresha said calmly.

There was a stricken silence. Then, for a reason that escaped Lily, she started to laugh.

"What's so funny?" Reni said. "She lied to me!"

"I know!" Lily said, sputtering. "But she's so — *honest* about it!"

Zooey burst into giggles, and even Suzy gave a nervous chuckle. Kresha was grinning like Ronald McDonald.

"Lily — she needz help," Kresha said. "You must be here, Reni."

Reni folded her arms across her chest. She had yet to sit down, even though Suzy kept inching the one empty beanbag chair toward her. "So as usual," Reni said, "it's all about Lily."

"Ya," Kresha said.

"But I'm sick of that!" Reni said. "That's why we all broke up in the first place!"

"No, Reni," Suzy said.

But Lily nodded, sending red curls in all directions. "She's right, Suzy. This is all my fault, and now I don't know what to do."

Reni was looking at Lily intently. "You admit you messed some things up?" she said.

"Yes!" Lily said.

Reni unfolded her arms. "Then I admit I messed some stuff up too. Lots of stuff."

"Like what?" Zooey said.

"No," Kresha said. "No now. Now we talk about Lily — her proplem."

At last Reni dropped into the beanbag. "What's going on?" she said.

With that one question, Lily's empty hole drew in its sides until it was no more than a crack. She and Reni would fill it up later, when they sorted things out. But right now, Reni was all about problem solving.

Wow, Lily thought. *That must be her gift.*

"Come on, Lil — dish," Reni said.

96

For a second, Lily felt uncertain again. "If I tell you guys, you have to promise not to say a word to anybody — and I mean *anybody* else — until I tell you it's okay." She glanced quickly at Reni. "I'm not trying to be bossy — it's just important. You'll see why. But do you promise?"

Everyone gave a serious nod. Even Reni. Then Lily started from the beginning and told the Girlz the whole story. When she got to the part about feeling like she was as bad as the ABCs were if she didn't reveal what she knew to Ms. Ferringer, Reni put up her hand.

"Lily," she said, "girl, there is only one thing to do."

"What?" Lily said.

"We got to pray — all of us — right now."

They got into their usual circle and held hands and talked to God like he was right there with them. Lily was sure he was.

It was so different from the day before, she thought, when she'd told Ian they should pray and he had told her he didn't pray. She added in a little prayer for him.

When they raised their heads, a plate of oatmeal cookies had magically appeared on the bottom step, along with a pitcher of grape juice. Everybody chattered and poured and chewed — while Reni sat scowling. It made Lily nervous — enough to say, "What's going on, Reni? Are you mad at me again?"

"No," she said. "I was just thinking."

"Uh-oh," Suzy said. Now *she* looked nervous.

Reni wrinkled her forehead. "You guys ever pray and then when you're done, you just know something?"

"You know something?" Lily said.

"Yeah — I think so." Reni gnawed on her bottom lip. "I'm thinking you better talk to a grown-up about this, Lily — " she said, " — before you decide what to do."

"You think?" Lily said. But she didn't even have to ask. She was already feeling relieved and planning what she was going to say to Mom and Dad.

Chapter
12

M om and Dad were talking about dollars and budgets and other adult-sounding things in Dad's study that evening when Lily poked her head in.

"Oh," she said. "You guys look busy. Will you tell me when we can talk?"

Dad slapped the checkbook closed, and Mom stuck her pen into the rooster-tail bun she had tied up on the top of her head.

"Right now," Dad said.

"Let me uncover a horizontal plane — there you go," Mom said. She dumped a stack of files that were on a chair onto the floor.

"Don't you have to finish what you were doing?" Lily said.

"Not until we take care of you," Dad said.

"Wow," Lily said.

"Did we say something amazing, and we didn't even know it?" Mom said.

"You know, just like that, what you're supposed to do. You don't even have to think about it." She sighed as she sat in the chair. "I wish I was like that."

"You will be, Lilliputian," Dad said. "You're much too hard on yourself."

"So what's up?" Mom said.

Although Lily had been practicing her presentation even in her head during supper when everybody else was expressing an opinion about the new bathroom, now that she was about to begin, she wasn't so sure how to. But then she remembered the Girlz, all praying with her today, and laughing again, and fighting over the last cookie.

"I have a real problem," she said. "And I need some advice."

Dad said, "Anything you need, Lilliputian. What's the deal?"

Once again Lily told the story, and once again she felt the empty space filling up with a kind of peace. Now, when Mom and Dad told her what to do, she could fill it up the rest of the way with a solution.

But when she was finished, Dad said, "So, what do you think you should do?"

"I don't know," Lily said, blinking. "I thought you guys would tell me."

"We could do that," Dad said, "but why? You already know."

"No, I don't!"

"Sure you do," Mom said. "That's the problem—you've already decided what's right to do. Now you're struggling with how to make everybody like it." She leaned toward Lily, and her mouth wasn't twitching. She looked as if she were talking to another grown-up. "No decision you make is ever going to please everybody. Only politicians try to do that. Real leaders decide *whom* they really have to please. And *who* is that?"

"God?"

"Bingo. What's it going to be, Lil?" Mom said. "Are you going to go for God's vote or the—what did you call them?—the ABCs?"

"I'm gonna do the God thing," Lily said. "I'm gonna tell Ms. Ferringer." She sighed through her nose. "But I'm never gonna get *anybody's* vote ever again. I'm getting out of politics. I don't have the gift to be a leader. Look how I messed everything up!"

"Leaders make mistakes all the time," Dad said. "That's not what determines whether you're a true leader or not. It's how you correct those mistakes."

"We need food for this," Mom said. "I hear some popcorn calling."

They adjourned to the kitchen, where Mom pulled a package out of the cabinet and pushed the necessary buttons on the microwave. The three of them talked about how Lily *was* going to fix things, and what was going to happen as a result. By the time they were finished — when Joe finally smelled the popcorn and followed his nose down to the kitchen — Lily was so tired she gave him her share and went to her room. As Dad said to her when she left, she had miles to go before she slept.

The first thing she did was pray. That took a while, but only because she had so much to say. It was easier now, though.

That didn't mean, however, that she wasn't nervous when she picked up the phone and dialed Ian's number. He answered on the first ring, and he sounded pretty happy that it was her. That is, until she broke the news to him.

"You're gonna mess everything up!" he fairly shouted into the phone.

"If you don't want me to mention your name, I won't."

"They're so gonna know we were in it together! I never shoulda let you talk me into even leaving that note."

Lily waited some more. Finally, after Ian had sighed about thirty times, he said, "If Ms. Ferringer doesn't ask about me, don't say anything. But if she does, you don't have to lie for me."

"Oh, I won't," Lily said.

Ian gave a snort. "Who knew you'd turn out to be such a goody-goody?"

"God, I guess," Lily said.

Right after that, they hung up.

Before they left the house the next morning, Mom and Dad prayed with Lily in her room. It helped to have that image in her mind as she climbed out of the van at school and went straight to Ms. Ferringer's room. She looked a little better than she had the day before, but the minute Lily broke the news to her, leaving Ian's name out of it, she seemed to scatter herself in ten different directions.

"Why do kids have to put me in this position?" she said to Lily. "I *so* don't have time for this right now." She put her fingers up to her forehead for a second, and then she blinked rapidly and turned back to Lily.

"Do you know exactly where the stuff is on the Internet so I can locate all of it without having to spend half the day doing it?"

"Yes," Lily said. "I can show you."

Ms. Ferringer stopped blinking and peered at her closely. "I had no idea you were even into computers," she said.

Lily drew in a big breath, but she didn't answer.

"Okay, show me," Ms. Ferringer said.

Somehow Lily got to the computer and, after Ms. Ferringer logged her on, fumbled her way into the Internet and found Benjamin's project. Ms. Ferringer studied it, and her eyes drooped with every word.

"I'll have to compare it with his paper," she said, almost to herself. "But I already know this is it. I must be the biggest idiot in the history of the teaching profession."

"Probably not the *biggest* one," Lily said.

"Thanks, Lily," Ms. Ferringer said. "That's all I need. You can go."

Lily nodded and picked up her backpack. As she left, she looked back at Ms. Ferringer. She was still staring at the computer screen.

You're too hard on yourself, Lily wanted to tell her. *You should try praying.*

In third period, Ian wrote Lily a note she was afraid to open. For once, she wished Mrs. Reinhold *would* catch it en route so Lily didn't have to read what it said.

But Ian's timing was perfect. When Mrs. Reinhold turned to write the assignment on the board, the note made its way straight to her. Tucking it behind her vocabulary notebook, she took the plunge.

Did you do it? it said. *Just nod if you did, and I won't come to fourth period today. Ian P.S. If I were you, I'd cut too.*

The thought of skipping a class sent chills up Lily's spine. She crumpled up the note and tossed it in the nearby trashcan. Then she looked at Ian and nodded without smiling. His eyes narrowed down so far, she could barely see them.

Ian didn't come to fourth period. Ms. Ferringer took the ABCs out into the hall again. And this time, they didn't return. Ms. Ferringer collected their backpacks for them and sent a couple of other kids down to the office with them.

"Why aren't they coming back?" Marcie said.

"Because they've been busted," Ms. Ferringer said. "And so will anybody else who cheats in my class. Is that understood?"

For the first time all year, Ms. Ferringer's room was silent. Some kids even nodded their heads as if they thought she meant it.

After lunch the list came out naming the kids who weren't going to be allowed to go to Friday's party. Only the teachers were supposed to see it, but Mr. Chester was an old-fashioned teacher; he posted it on his bulletin board.

"That's, like, so embarrassing!" Marcie wailed — because, of course, her name was on it.

"You should have kept your nose clean," Mr. Chester said. "Get out last night's homework."

"What does that mean?" Marcie said, lower lip stuck out like a sofa.

"Do you have your homework?" he said.

"No."

"That's what that means."

To Lily's surprise, no one came up to her the rest of the day to complain about the stupid requirements for the party. In fact, both of her classes were unusually quiet that afternoon, as if people were stunned that the school had gone through with it.

The surprise came the next morning when Lily got a note during her first-period class telling her to report to the office. She wasn't disturbed as she sailed down the hall. It was probably just Mr. Tanini wanting to make sure all the details were taken care of.

She did *get* disturbed — right down to her stomach — when she saw Ian there, along with Ms. Ferringer, and neither one of them looked like congratulations were in order.

"Sit down, would you, Lily?" Mr. Tanini said.

Is something wrong? she asked Ian with her eyes.

He glared at her briefly and then gave Mr. Tanini a smile. It looked like the plastic mouth in the Mr. Potato Head kit.

"Something has come to my attention that I need to address with the three of you," Mr. Tanini said.

From the looks of Ms. Ferringer, he had already addressed it with her.

"This morning, Ms. Ferringer brought me this." Mr. Tanini held up a piece of paper. "It's a list which she found on her computer — a list she says only you two could have made."

"We've made lists on her computer," Ian said. "That's how we planned all our stuff." He turned to Ms. Ferringer. "You told us we could. You even logged us on." He looked back at Mr. Tanini. "You have to have a password to get on, and I don't know it."

Lily winced. If she had been Mr. Tanini, she would have been more suspicious of Ian than ever. He sounded like he was begging for his life.

"What's wrong with the list Ms. Ferringer found?" Lily said. "All we did was put down ideas we came up with, and you gave us permission for all of those."

"Really?" he said. "These ideas are about the party — and I certainly didn't give permission for these."

Lily felt her eyebrows meeting in the middle. She could see Ian's upper lip sweating, even from where she was sitting.

"Let me enlighten you," Mr. Tanini said. He cocked his head back slightly and read through the bottoms of his glasses. "One. Play the

EMINEM CD — at top volume. Two. Booby trap the gift for Mr. Tanini so it shoots whipped cream in his face when he opens it. Three. At 2:45, start a food fight." Mr. Tanini stopped reading. "Is that enough to refresh your memories? There's more if you need it."

"We never wrote that," Lily said. Her stomach was slowly tying itself into a bow, but her voice came out clear and steady.

"No, we didn't," Ian said. "At least *I* didn't."

Lily looked at Ian. He was working an innocent expression onto his face.

"I'm in a quandary here, people," Mr. Tanini said. "I don't want to believe that either one or both of you made up this plan and intended to carry it out. But where did it come from?"

"I don't know," Lily said.

"Me neither," Ian said.

Mr. Tanini pressed the bridge of his nose with two fingers before he spoke again. "I don't usually pay too much attention to rumors," he said finally. "But I started hearing about some of this yesterday afternoon, just in passing, even before Ms. Ferringer brought this to me. I heard talk of this — " He referred to the list. "This EMINEM being played. They said you, Lily, were hoarding it in your locker, waiting to slip it in."

"No, that's not true," Lily said, her voice still unwavering.

"All right, then," Mr. Tanini said, "suppose we go have a look."

They all got up, and Mr. Tanini led the way out the door. Ian caught Lily by the arm as she started to follow.

"Is it still in there?" he said quietly.

"What?"

"The EMINEM CD."

Lily started to shake her head, but she froze abruptly.

Lee's CD — the one they'd pulled that Friday. It was still there in the bottom of her locker. And Mr. Tanini was headed right for it.

Chapter 13

A number of plans went through Lily's head as she followed Mr. Tanini, Ms. Ferringer, and Ian up the stairs. But each idea — maybe she could run in the other direction, leap into the nearest trashcan, conveniently forget her combination — skittered out the minute she thought of it. *I didn't even do anything! What do I need a plan for?*

When they were within a few yards of the locker area, Ian slowed down until Lily was right beside him. He opened that little hole in the side of his mouth again.

"When you're taking stuff out of your locker, pick up the CD and stick it in one of your books or something," he said.

"Why would I do that?" Lily whispered. "It's not even my CD."

"You think they're gonna believe that?"

"Well — yeah."

Ian shook his head and rolled his eyes. "Do what you want," he said, still out of the little hole, "but leave my name out of it."

"But — "

"Problem, kids?" Mr. Tanini said. He was standing at the end of the row of lockers, hands on hips, looking suspicious.

"No—there's no problem," Lily said. She stepped away from Ian, and, with a huge lump in her throat, she went up to Mr. Tanini. She had never realized before how tall he was.

"Mr. Tanini," she said, "you're gonna find that CD in my locker because we had to pull it out at the last minute on Friday. I just never got it back to the kid who owns it."

"I thought those decisions were made way ahead of time," Mr. Tanini said, looking directly at Ms. Ferringer.

Lily wanted to bite her tongue off. No matter what she said, she was going to get somebody in trouble.

And then she could almost hear Mom's voice, saying, *No decision you're ever going to make is going to please everybody. Whom do you have to please?*

Lily took a deep breath. "We never told Ms. Ferringer what happened with the CD," she said, "and we should have. But that list she found wasn't ours."

"But no one else had access to Ms. Ferringer's computer, Lily." Mr. Tanini lowered his head closer to her. "Unless you know something she doesn't."

Lily had to gulp in another huge breath. "I think I do," she said.

She could feel Ian poking her, hard, in the back. But he wasn't the one she had to please.

"One day I got to Ms. Ferringer's room before school," Lily said to Mr. Tanini, "and these two kids were already in there, using her computer."

Mr. Tanini raised his eyebrows. "And you didn't tell Ms. Ferringer?"

"I thought she knew. I thought she let them in since the door was already open."

Mr. Tanini looked at Ms. Ferringer, who was blinking hard. Lily felt sorry for her, but there was nothing she could do about it. She had to do what was right.

"I do remember Lily and Ian being in the room when I got there, and I thought I'd locked it," Ms. Ferringer said. "But I was in a rush — I'm always in a rush." Her voice fell. "I didn't pursue it."

Mr. Tanini turned back to Lily. "Who were these students?" he said.

Ian cleared his throat — a high-pitched noise that made him sound as if he'd been pinched.

"It was Ashley Adamson and Benjamin Weeks," Lily said. "They were at the computer when I got there. When they saw me, they turned it off and left."

"Was anybody else with you? Did anyone else see them?"

Lily shook her head. Ian was pushing her so hard in the back, it was all she could do not to turn around and shout, *I'm leaving your name out of it — so chill!*

"Didn't the whole thing seem strange to you?" Mr. Tanini said.

"It did when we tried to get on the computer, and we saw that we had to have a password. But I thought Ms. Ferringer had logged Ashley and Ben on and then left, just like she'd always done for us."

"But I hadn't," Ms. Ferringer said. "I'm sorry, Lily," she said. "But I never logged them on or gave them the password. It couldn't have been them — or anybody else. I keep that password locked in my desk at all times. And the *only* people I ever typed it in for were the officers."

Lily was sure she saw tears shining in Ms. Ferringer's eyes. She was telling the truth, Lily thought, and just like Lily, she probably hated doing it right now. The only thing that would make it better for both of them would be if Ian would say he'd seen Ashley and Benjamin leaving when he came down the hall and that Lily had told him about their being there.

But Ian stood quietly, hands in his pockets, his face as innocent as if he'd just walked in on the conversation.

Wow, Lily said to herself, *he doesn't even look a little bit guilty.* It was easy to guess who he had to please.

Mr. Tanini ran his hand over his bald head as if he could somehow stir up the right thought. "You're making a serious charge, Lily," he said. "Just like you did when you pointed out that those students had pirated their projects off of the Internet. Only this time, it seems it's your word against theirs. Shall I ask them if they did this?"

Lily went cold, but she nodded. "You could do that, and it wouldn't change my mind. But I know they aren't going to admit it."

"I think it has to be done, though," Mr. Tanini said. "It's only fair — unless you want to retract your statement about seeing them on the computer."

Lily shook her head. Behind her, Ian cleared his throat again. "Uh, Mr. Tanini," he said. "Do you have to mention Lily's name when you ask them if they did this? They could make it pretty hard on her."

My name? Lily thought. *Suddenly you're all worried about my name?*

"That's okay," she said. "You can tell them it was me if you want to. I'm not lying — so I don't have anything to be afraid of."

Mr. Tanini sighed heavily, the way Dad did when he had to ground somebody. "I'll get back to you by third period," he said to Ms. Ferringer.

She nodded miserably.

"Let me sign your passes," he said, holding out his hand to Lily. "You two kids can go on back to class."

Lily didn't look at Ian as she handed her hall pass to Mr. Tanini, and she hurried off so that he couldn't catch up to her. She blinked away a threatening blur. *I'm definitely getting out of politics,* she thought. *This hurts way too much.*

Somehow she got through second period without breaking down, but by the time she got to Mrs. Reinhold's class, she was barely holding it in. It was a good thing Reni and Suzy were there in the hall outside the room.

"What's going on?" Reni said. "I heard you and Ian got hauled to the office first period."

"You're not in trouble, Lily, are you?" Suzy said.

Even though Lily had to give them the abbreviated version of the story, they looked horrified by the time she wrapped it up, and they hurried into the classroom. Lily sank into her seat, behind Ashley's empty one, feeling a little better. She'd never known two terrified faces that matched hers could be so healing.

The bell rang, and Lily was getting out her English homework when it dawned on her that Ashley wasn't there. She glanced around while Mrs. Reinhold checked the roll. Neither were Chelsea, Bernadette, or Benjamin. It certainly struck Mrs. Reinhold as odd.

"Does anyone know the whereabouts of Ashley et al.?" she said.

"Huh?" Marcie said.

"I do not respond to 'huh,'" Mrs. Reinhold said.

As she went on to explain what "et al." meant, Lily concentrated on getting her heart to stop pounding. Even from across the room, she could tell Reni was scribbling out a Girlz Gram.

"Ashley and them got called to the office last period," Marcie said to Mrs. Reinhold. "I think it was about — "

"Never you mind," Mrs. Reinhold said. "This is not an arena for conjecturing."

"Mrs. Reinhold," Marcie said, "how come I never know what you're talking about?"

Lily looked over at Ian. He was laughing and exchanging nods with Lee as if all was right with the world. Could it be, she wondered, that he didn't care what happened as long as his name didn't get dragged into it?

Just then, the door opened, and the ABCs came in. Lily could read their faces. Every one of them said, *This time we got away with it.*

As Ashley parked herself importantly in her desk and glanced back at Lily, Ashley's face also said: *And this time, we took somebody down with us.*

It didn't take long to find out what she meant by that. Mrs. Reinhold picked up the pass Benjamin had dropped on her desk and said, "Lily. Ian. Suzy. Lee. You four are wanted in the office."

"Busted," Ashley murmured.

Lily barely heard her. She was worried about Suzy, who hardly seemed to be able to get herself out of her desk. Lily grabbed her hand as soon as they were out in the hall.

"Don't worry," Lily said to her. "You haven't done anything wrong."

"I'm scared for *you*," Suzy said.

Once again, somebody sharing the fear was enough. And that was something Ian had never done. Lee and Ian walked ahead of them, muttering to each other but behaving as if they weren't headed for the principal's office.

Mr. Tanini ushered them into his office, where Zooey was already gnawing on her fingernails. Lily sat down beside her and patted the chair on her other side for Suzy. Between them, she could whisper, "We've got nothing to worry about. Just pray."

From the look on Mr. Tanini's face, "nothing to worry about" was probably a little optimistic, but Lily felt like her first job was to keep Suzy from passing out and Zooey from consuming her cuticles.

"I've been very impressed with the work you all have done so far as seventh-grade officers," Mr. Tanini said. "So I am more disappointed than I would normally be to discover that we have a situation on our hands." He ran his hand across his head. *He's doing a lot of that today,* Lily thought. Probably if he'd had any hair, he would have been twirling it around his finger the way Ms. Ferringer did.

Mr. Tanini went through an explanation of what had happened with Ian and Lily that morning. Lily could hear Zooey swallowing a big tear-lump.

Then he folded his arms across his chest. "So last period I called the 'accused' in here and questioned them at length. Every one of them denies that he or she was ever in the room the morning Lily says she saw

Ben and Ashley using Ms. Ferringer's computer. And Chelsea and Bernadette say their friends never mentioned anything about it to them."

Nobody said anything. Mr. Tanini looked at Lily. "You couldn't have been mistaken?" he said.

"No, sir."

Mr. Tanini studied the floor for a moment. Finally he said, "I have Lily's word against theirs. Without any hard evidence, I can't say who is lying—though obviously someone is." He shook his head. "I don't think I have much choice but to cancel the party."

It was the first time Ian had looked the least bit alarmed. His head came up, and his glasses teetered on the bridge of his nose.

"But that's not fair!" he said. "It's all planned!"

"*What* is all planned?" Mr. Tanini said. He picked up the list from Ms. Ferringer and waved it. "This?"

"We didn't make that plan," Ian said. "You know how hard we worked to get this all together. We'll be *killed* if it doesn't come off."

"I'm sorry. I can't take any chances on any of this happening."

"But it's not going to!"

Mr. Tanini put up his hand. "What reassurance do I have?"

"You have our word," Ian said.

Your word, Ian? Lily thought. *How can he trust your word?*

"Sorry, folks," Mr. Tanini said. "The party is off. I'll notify the teachers." He held out his hand. "Let me sign your passes so you can go back to class."

He initialed Ian's and Lee's first. When Lily and Suzy and Zooey got out to the hall, they were just in time to hear Ian say to Lee, "I'm never going to class again! This is gonna be all over the school by lunch. We even show our faces, and we're dog meat."

The word was out before fourth period was over. The only people in class who didn't look upset about it were the ABCs. Reni glared at them so hard, Lily was sure they were all going to end up with holes drilled in the backs of their heads.

"I wrote you a note in third period," she said to Lily, "but you got called out before I could get it to you."

"What did it say?" Lily said "Only — if it was bad, don't tell me. I can't take any more bad news."

"It just said, like, what's wrong and do I need to kick somebody's rear?"

In spite of all the things that were dragging her mouth down at the corners, Lily laughed. "You wouldn't kick somebody's rear!"

"Yes, I would! I mean, not, like, really kick them — but I'll help you fight this."

"I can't fight it," Lily said. "It's my word against theirs."

Reni stretched her neck up. "You can't just lay down and die, girl! You got to fight for what's right."

"How?" Lily said.

"I don't know," Reni said, setting her face stubbornly, "but we'll figure out something. We always do."

Reni whipped a couple of Girlz Gram forms out of her backpack and began to write. "Here," she said, "write one to Zooey. Tell her we're meeting at lunch."

"But what about your orchestra practice?" Lily said. "And what about Monique?"

Reni looked a little sheepish. "I wasn't exactly honest about that. I kind of used Monique to make you jealous. But could we talk about it later? We got to get on this — the party's not that far off."

"I don't think it's gonna happen, Reni," Lily said.

"Oh, yes it is. *That's* what we gotta work on, girl."

All the Girlz were there at lunch, and they huddled together at their table to block out the angry glares that were being fired Lily's way.

"All right, everybody," Reni said, "think of ways we can prove that Ashley and her pals stole Ms. Ferringer's password, got on her computer, and messed everything up."

Zooey, Kresha, and Suzy all stared at her blankly.

"I'm not good at this," Zooey said. "That's not my gift thing like it is yours."

"Gift thing?" Reni said. "What are you talking about?"

"I don't know," Zooey said. "It's that thing Lily talks about all the time."

Reni turned to look at Lily, who was already nodding with the first glimmer of hope she'd felt all day.

"Yeah!" Lily said. "We could all use our gifts — you know, like the best thing we do — and see what we come up with."

"I don't get it," Suzy said.

"Your gift is all about writing stuff down," Lily said. "Look through your notes from all the meetings. See if there's a clue in there."

"So what do I do?" Zooey said.

It took Lily a few seconds, and then it came to her. "Look at the pictures you've taken. Maybe you caught something. I saw them do that on TV one time."

"Me, Lily?" Kresha said.

But before Lily could answer her, Suzy looked up from her notebook and waved her hand.

"What?" Reni said.

"Does this help?" Suzy said. "I wrote down that at our *first* meeting, Ms. Ferringer was looking for her keys the whole time."

"What's that got to do with anything?" Zooey said.

But Lily and Reni were already looking at each other and nodding excitedly.

"They took her keys and used them to get into her desk!" Lily said. "She said that's where she kept the password."

"And that's how they got into the room too," Suzy said.

"Yikes, you guys," Lily said. "I think I have an idea." She grinned at the Girlz. "And I think it'll let us *all* use our gifts."

Chapter
14

The Girlz polished their plan in time for Lily to go and find Ms. Ferringer before lunch was over. She located her on hall duty, wandering up and down as if she'd just lost everything. When Lily explained their plan to her, Ms. Ferringer stopped blinking. Best of all, she agreed to help.

In fifth period that day, Reni started the plan rolling. When the class got into study groups, Reni maneuvered her way right over to the group next to the one the ABCs formed with their desks. Lily made it a point to be on the other side of the room.

Once everyone was settled, Reni let her voice rise obnoxiously above Mr. Chester's approved volume level and said to the kids in her group, "I know somebody who's gonna get a hundred on that geography quiz we're having tomorrow."

"What geography quiz?" somebody said.

Lily sneaked a glance over the top of her math book. Ashley was staring openly at Reni from the next group.

"We're having a pop quiz tomorrow," Reni said.

"How do you know?" Ashley said.

Reni let her gaze shift deliberately over to Lily. "Oh, I just heard it. And I bet the person who told me is gonna get a hundred."

"Why?" Bernadette said.

All of the ABCs were completely zoned in on Reni by now, and Mr. Chester was beginning to stir in his desk chair.

Hurry up, Reni, Lily thought, *before Mr. Chester tells you to hush up.*

"Because," Reni said, tossing her beaded braids with a clack. "She got into Ms. Ferringer's desk drawer and found out where she keeps the answer keys."

"But Ms. Ferringer keeps her desk locked!" Chelsea said.

The ABCs all whirled their heads around to glare at Chelsea.

"This girl is sly," Reni said. "She has her ways. I'd study if I were you guys."

"There's an awful lot of chatter going on over there," Mr. Chester said. "And I don't think it's about solving for *x.*"

"Sorry, Mr. Chester," Bernadette said sweetly — and then leaned in to whisper to her group.

Lily and Reni exchanged satisfied glances. So far, so good.

Lily was pulling books out of her locker that afternoon after sixth period when Ian came up to her. Lily felt squirmy inside. It seemed strange not to know what to say to him when he had always been so easy to talk to.

"What was that all about in math today?" he said. "Reni talking about a pop quiz in Ms. Ferringer's class and somebody knowing the answers. What's she pulling?"

"Nothing," Lily said. "She's my friend, and she's honest — and she's helping me."

"Do what?"

"Carry out a plan," Lily said. "Tomorrow morning, before school, we're going to prove that Ben and Ashley know how to get into Ms. Ferringer's computer — which we wouldn't *have* to do if you had just spoken up — " Lily stopped and turned back to her locker. "Never mind," she said. "You wouldn't want to get involved. You might lose your popularity or something."

She could feel Ian watching her for another moment. Then he walked away.

That night, Lily told Mom and Dad about the Girlz' plan while they nodded their approval.

"Now, Lilliputian," Dad said when she was finished. "Don't be too disappointed if Mr. Tanini doesn't change his mind, even if your plan does work."

She shrugged. "I just wanna do the right thing, that's all."

"I'll say this." Mom put her arm around Lily's shoulders. "I think you really are using your gift of leadership."

"Wow," Lily said. "Just when I figure out I'm not really meant to be a leader after all, that's when you tell me it's okay to be one."

Dad chewed on the earpiece of his glasses, his eyes twinkling. "We're not the ones telling you, Lilliputian."

Mom's mouth twitched. "Lil — you go, girl. We'll be praying for you."

By 7:30 the next morning, Reni, Lily, and Suzy were gathered on the bench, half praying together, half picturing Zooey upstairs in Ms. Ferringer's closet with her camera. Every few seconds, they glanced up at Kresha, who was stationed on the stairs ready to give signals. Lily couldn't help smiling as she remembered how excited Kresha had been when Lily had told her that her gift was being invisible to the ABCs.

"They always act like you're not there," Lily had told her. "Like they can say anything they want around you because they think you can't understand English."

"Psst!" Kresha hissed now. She held up two fingers — the arranged signal that meant Benjamin had arrived. He was number two in the alphabetical order of the ABCs.

Lily, Suzy, and Reni waited, clinging to each other's hands, as Kresha disappeared. She was back in a flash, nodding to them.

"Here we go," Lily whispered to the Girlz.

Then they tiptoed quietly up the steps and stationed themselves just around the corner from Ms. Ferringer's classroom. Kresha pointed down Ms. F's hall.

Ashley and Bernadette and Chelsea are right there, Lily thought. *God, if this is what's supposed to happen — please let it happen, okay?*

Apparently God was up for letting it happen, because Kresha gave another signal, directed down the hall. Lily could hear Ms. Ferringer's heels tapping the floor as she headed for her classroom. And just as they'd hoped, there was a rustling around the corner as the ABCs moved from their places, ready to head Ms. Ferringer off before she could go into her room and catch Ben.

Lily jerked her head at Suzy and Reni. The three of them burst around the corner, elbowed their way ahead of Ashley, Bernadette, and Chelsea, and stood in front of them.

"What?" Chelsea said.

She tried to dodge Reni, but Reni planted her feet firmly and stuck out her hand so that Chelsea ran right into it. Lily did the same to Ashley. She didn't dare move her eyes to see if Suzy was okay with Bernadette. They'd assigned her to Suzy because Bernadette was the least likely of the ABCs to throw a punch.

Judging from the way Ashley's nostrils were flaring, she wasn't going to let Lily hold her back for long — so it was a major relief to hear Ms. Ferringer shout from inside her room, "What are *you* doing in here?"

Lily held her breath and listened for Benjamin's answer. Instead, Ms. Ferringer's door flew open, and Ben bolted out. The instant they saw him, Ashley, Bernadette, and Chelsea shoved the Girlz out of the way and took off after Benjamin, who was wasting no time disappearing down the hall.

"Let's go!" Reni said.

The three Girlz tore into Ms. Ferringer's room. Just as Lily had hoped, Zooey was standing there beaming. In her hand was a Polaroid snapshot.

"Let's see!" Reni said.

Zooey handed over the picture and turned to Suzy, who had at least a hundred questions for Zooey to make sure she was okay. Lily crowded behind Reni and looked over her shoulder.

There it was, all right — a perfect photograph of Benjamin with his hand in Ms. Ferringer's open desk drawer.

"Where's Depu — I mean, Officer Horn?" Suzy said, looking nervously toward the door.

"You can count on Deputy Dog," Ms. Ferringer said. "She promised me she'd nab them the minute they got out of here. May I see that picture?"

Reni handed it over, and the Girlz watched as Ms. Ferringer studied it.

"Did we get 'em good?" Zooey said, still beaming.

Ms. Ferringer twirled a curl. "I'm not sure, guys," she said. "You can tell he's digging around in my drawer, but there's nothing to show he was getting my answer key — or that he unlocked the drawer in the first place."

"Well — is the answer key still in there?" Reni said.

"Oh," Ms. Ferringer said. She gave her deep throaty laugh. "Du-uh!"

All of them crowded to the desk and hovered over Ms. Ferringer as she rummaged through her drawer.

"I don't see it in here," she said.

"Is that good?" Zooey said.

"It could be," Ms. Ferringer said.

The door opened then, and everyone jumped. Kresha appeared, wearing a grin the shape of an orange slice. She swept out a hand with a flourish to announce the entrance of Deputy Dog. *Her* smile was square and satisfied.

"Mission accomplished — almost," she said.

"What do you mean 'almost'?" Lily said.

"The three young ladies are in custody," Deputy Dog said. "But our boy got away."

Lily sagged, but Deputy Dog hooked her thumbs into her belt in that way that meant business. "Not to worry, Robbins," she said. "We'll get him."

But probably not soon enough to catch him with the answer key in his pocket, Lily thought. *I think we can forget the party.*

"Don't give up, guys," Ms. Ferringer said. "You at least accomplished something." She let go of the curl she'd been twirling and touched Lily's arm. "I'm sorry I didn't outright believe you, Lily I know the quality person you are — I should have just taken your word for it."

"That's okay," Lily said. "I don't blame you for not wanting to cross those kids."

"They can flat be mean, that's for sure," Reni said.

But Ms. Ferringer shook her head. "No — I'm a teacher. I'm not supposed to be afraid of the kids."

Still, when the door opened again, she jumped. So did the Girlz. And then Lily felt her mouth falling open, practically exposing her tonsils.

Standing in the doorway was Ian — holding Benjamin by the arm.

"*Hel*-lo," Deputy Dog said. "Just the man I was looking for."

She was behind Ben in two steps, taking over his arm where Ian left off. Ian came over to the Girlz and Ms. Ferringer.

"How did he know to catch Ben?" Reni whispered to Lily.

Lily didn't answer. She was watching Ian dig into his pocket and pull out a folded piece of paper. When Ms. Ferringer's eyes started blinking at nine hundred blinks per second, Lily knew what it was.

"I saw him running down the stairs, and I followed him into the restroom," Ian said, breathing like a large locomotive. "He was about to flush that paper down the toilet, when I grabbed it from him."

119

"Nice work, guy," Deputy Dog said. "You want a job?" She gave another square grin and jerked her head from Ben to the door. "Come on, dude. Let's take a walk."

When they were gone, the Girlz could only stare at each other — all except Lily, who was looking at Ian. He was making a careful study of his left foot.

You ended up being the hero, Lily thought. *And you don't deserve it —*

But Lily stopped her thoughts in their tracks. She was pretty sure that wasn't what a leader did. And for the first time, she really, really felt like one.

"This is my answer key," Ms. Ferringer said, tapping the piece of paper Ian had given her. "You guys got them."

"Well, Ian got them," Lily said.

Reni jabbed her with an elbow, but Lily went on. "If Ian hadn't caught Ben before he flushed it down the john, it still would have been mostly our word against his — again."

"Not quite," Ms. Ferringer said. She reached inside her grade book and pulled out another piece of paper. "This is the real answer key," she said. "The one Ben took was all wrong. I would have caught them the minute I checked their papers."

"*You* did that?" Reni said, staring at Ms. Ferringer.

It was Lily's turn to jab Reni in the ribs. Tact definitely wasn't Reni's gift.

The rumors were flying by the time first period started, and they were such a tangled mess that Lily stopped listening to them. The version that Deputy Dog had held Benjamin at gunpoint was the last straw.

But when Mr. Tanini interrupted classes over the intercom at the beginning of third period to make a special announcement, Lily listened to every syllable.

"Through an unfortunate series of events a few days ago," Mr. Tanini said, "I felt that it was necessary to cancel today's Christmas party and to hesitate before honoring any more of the seventh-grade officers' requests for special programs and projects."

He paused for a moment, and Lily could feel everyone turning to stare at her. She expected her face to go blotchy any second, but to her surprise — it didn't.

"However, new information has come to light," Mr. Tanini went on. "Information that clears the names of the seventh-grade class officers — Lily Robbins, Ian Collins, Lee Ohara, Suzy Wheeler, and Zooey Hoffman. They are fine young leaders, and I think it is only fair to allow them to go on with the party today as planned."

In spite of Mrs. Reinhold rapping her pen on her desk, a cheer went up in the classroom that drowned out whatever else Mr. Tanini might be saying. Lily sat like a statue while other kids patted her on the back and tried to high-five her. As if he could hear the students all the way down in the office, Mr. Tanini waited until the din died down to say, "Teachers — please send the seventh-grade officers to see me right now. I won't keep them for long. Thank you."

"May we go, Mrs. Reinhold?" Lily said.

"Of course you may," Mrs. Reinhold said. "I'm very proud of all of you. You're fine young leaders."

Lily and Suzy followed Lee to the door. Just behind her, she heard Ian say, "Uh, Mrs. Reinhold?"

"Yes, Ian," Mrs. Reinhold said.

"Um — what you said — about being leaders: that's not true for me."

"Oh?"

Lily let Lee go out ahead of her and stood, frozen.

"Yeah," Ian said. "I'm not the real leader. Lily — she's the leader."

Then Ian headed for the door with his head down.

"Wanna walk with us down to the office?" Lily said to him.

He stared at her for a long few seconds. "You don't have to," he said.

"I know," Lily said. "But I want to."

"Okay," Ian said. He punched his hands into his pockets and walked several steps behind her. When they got to the corner, Lily dropped back and fell into step beside him.

"Sorry I didn't speak up for ya," Ian said.

"Me too," Lily said. "But we all make mistakes."

"Huh," Ian said. "You never do."

"You gotta be kidding!" Lily said. "I was a terrible leader until I figured out it can't ever be all about me."

Ian's brown eyes looked puzzled behind his lenses. "Who *is* it all about, then?"

"It's mostly about God," Lily said.

"Oh," he said.

He looked a little disappointed. But that was okay. Maybe they could talk about that later. Meanwhile — the seventh-grade class officers had a party to pull off.

Us — Lily thought — *and God.*

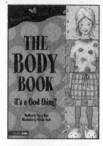
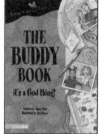

NIV Young Women of Faith Bible
GENERAL EDITOR SUSIE SHELLENBERGER

Designed just for girls ages 8-12, the *NIV Young Women of Faith Bible* not only has a trendy, cool look, it's packed with fun to read in-text features that spark interest, provide insight, highlight key foundational portions of Scripture, and more. Discover how to apply God's word to your everyday life with the *NIV Young Women of Faith Bible*.

Hardcover 0-310-91394-2
Softcover 0-310-70278-X
Slate Leather–Look™ 0-310-70485-5
Periwinkle Leather–Look™ 0-310-70486-3

NEW!

NEW!

Available now at your local bookstore!

Zonder**kidz**.

Coming August 2002

Rough & Rugged Lily (Book 9)
Softcover 0-310-70260-7

The Year 'Round Holiday Book companion

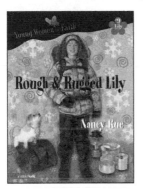

Lily Speaks! (Book 10)
Softcover 0-310-70262-3

The Values & Virtues Book companion

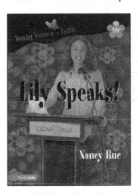

The Year 'Round Holiday Book
... It's a God Thing!
Softcover 0-310-70256-9

Rough & Rugged Lily companion

The Values & Virtues Book
... It's a God Thing!
Softcover 0-310-70257-7

Lily Speaks! companion

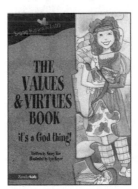

Zonder**kidz**™

We want to hear from you. Please send your comments about this book to us in care of the address below. Thank you.

Zonder**kidz**™

Grand Rapids, MI 49530
www.zonderkidz.com